Dé

THE SERENITY MURDER

A LUCA MYSTERY CRIME THRILLER

A LUCA MYSTERY
BOOK 3

DAN PETROSINI

Print ISBN: 978-1-960286-05-5

Naples, FL

Library of Congress Control Number: 2023901506

OTHER BOOKS BY DAN

Complicit Witness

Push Back

Ambition Cliff

ACKNOWLEDGMENTS

Special thanks to Julie, Stephanie and Jennifer for their love and support, and thanks to Squad Sergeant Craig Perrilli for his counsel on the real world of law enforcement. He helps me keep it real.

NAPLES, FLORIDA

1

GIDEON BRIGHTHOUSE

I HEARD THE YACHT REVERSE ENGINES AS IT MANEUVERED into the dock and got off my lounge chair. Walking to the end of the wraparound deck, I wanted to be sure it was Marilyn. Sure enough, she stepped on the dock, trailed by two white-uniformed deckhands laden down with the day's bounty. Her shopping addiction was the only thing that hadn't changed since the day we met.

Knowing her temporary high would ebb once things were put away, I bathed in the beauty of Keewaydin Island for a minute longer before heading to the main house. Padding down the stone path, I surveyed my slice of paradise; it was the only place I felt at peace since the panic attacks started. I didn't mind spending days alone here; in fact, I relished it. During the days I'd listen to music on the deck, peruse art books, and alternate dips in the pool with swims in the shimmering gulf. The days would melt away, and when the sun began to ease into the horizon, I'd have dinner on the deck before heading to hang out in the art building.

It was a fulfilling existence, and the fact was, I'd never had a panic attack on Keewaydin in all the years I'd lived there, even after my heart attack. However, once I was off the island, all bets were off. I prayed the streak would stay intact today with the stress of confronting Marilyn.

The main home, dubbed Serenity House, was a light blue, two-story building in the Key West style. It was capped with a silver-gray metal roof and sported generous porches on each level. Over the past five years I'd spent less and less time in Serenity House. Eventually I traded sleeping there for the guesthouse by the pool when things with Marilyn deteriorated about two years ago.

Reflecting on our relationship, I honestly could say I don't know how we went from happily in love to hating each other. It wasn't me, at least at first, who'd upended things. My career as a senior advisor to Senator White was peaking when Marilyn and I met. It had taken me a while to find something satisfying to do outside the art world. Though politics and art are universes apart, I was able to use my creativity during the campaign and quickly rose through the ranks.

The combination of power and access was a drug that energized our relationship. While we both relished the endless stream of events, parties, and White House state dinners, I didn't realize at the time that it was central to our marriage. When Senator White stumbled into a scandal during his bid for reelection, Marilyn distanced herself from me. I initially misread it, believing she was disappointed and that it would pass. However, as polls showed White trailing the upstart challenger, she became increasingly testy and changed into an ice queen before the last ballots were counted. We never really recovered.

I climbed the stairs to the porch where, shaded and aided by a steady gulf breeze, it was twenty degrees cooler. Despite the Boggs family's formality and wealth, the home had a welcoming, relaxed feel. It was that vibe that had me convincing Marilyn to move from Port Royal to the island. She initially resisted, but later agreed, saying it was to please me, but I knew what ultimately swayed her was the fact that no one else lived on their own private island. She used the isolation card to justify spending fifteen million on a Gulf Shore Boulevard penthouse and added a Fifth Avenue apartment that checked in at three million. It was excessive and sickening at times, but there was no doubt it was convenient and fun as all hell for a little while.

Marilyn was in the kitchen giving instruction to Shell, a housekeeper. It was a Tuesday. The household staff were off Wednesdays, as Marilyn wanted the house empty for her midweek interludes. I stopped and admired the Jasper Johns piece that hung over the white limestone fireplace. The painting, known as *Map*, was a vibrant, richly worked expression that defined Johns' move from abstract to things more concrete. It was one of the first pieces I recommended buying, and it had risen in value like all the others, providing me with a tiny sword to defend my so-called laziness.

Before I could fully absorb a whimsical flower painting by Murakami, Ruby, another housekeeper in black uniform and crepe-soled shoes, came down the stairs. Knowing our greeting would alert Marilyn to my presence, I walked into the kitchen. Mid-sentence, Shell nodded and left.

Her back to me, Marilyn was outfitted in deep blue athletic wear that clung to her thin frame. The silence was broken when she turned on her latest obsession, a fancy juicer. It bought me thirty seconds to reconsider, and I had to inch forward to prevent myself from leaving.

Produce duly liquefied, she turned and said, "My, my, what—the air conditioning's broken in the pool house?"

"We have to talk."

"About what?"

"Us."

She stuck a straw in the green soup and took a sip before saying, "Now is not a good time. I've got a yoga class with Gerard in a few minutes."

"Come on, Marilyn, we both know it's not working."

Green eyes glaring, she said, "Perhaps if you engaged in a useful activity instead of moping around the property like a lunatic, things might be better."

"That's not fair. You know how hard it is for me to leave Keewaydin."

She muttered, "How convenient and pitiful."

I wanted to shove the drink down her throat. "You think so? Well, did you ever consider the attacks I suffer started right after the first time you cheated on me?"

"So, it's my fault you're dysfunctional?"

"Please, I don't want to argue."

"Fine by me."

Marilyn took a long sip, set the drink down and walked out, saying, "I got to go."

I trailed after her. "Come on, Marilyn. Can't we talk this over?"

"I don't like this arrangement any more than you do, Gideon."

She threw the door open to a mirror-walled studio and headed to a rack filled with colorful mats. She grabbed a red one and unrolled it as I said, "Okay, okay. Why don't we negotiate a divorce settlement?"

Putting her hands on her hips, she said, "What do you want in a so-called settlement, Gideon?"

I couldn't look her in the eye and peered over her head at the endless mirror images of the two of us. A tightness grew in my chest.

Smiling, she said, "Tell me, I'm so interested to understand what it is that my beloved Gideon desires. It's certainly not sex, is it now?"

She was right. I'd found myself sufficiently revolted by her that we hadn't had sex in three years.

"I don't know why you always have to be so, so . . . cruel." I couldn't get enough air in. "Just forget it."

"Don't run away now, Gideon. You started this, so let's finish it."

Sucking in a deep breath, I said, "I don't want anything but the right to live here, and some of my art."

"Your art? You mean the pieces the trust paid for?" She laughed. "I don't think so. And as far as the island goes, that's completely out of the question."

My mouth was bone-dry. "So, you'd rather go on living this way?"

"I'll take the hit and agree to a divorce, but you'll only get what the prenuptial provides. That's all you're entitled to, and I'm not giving up a dollar more, especially to you."

Her old man, Martin Boggs, founded America's third-largest mutual fund company and had built a multibillion-dollar fortune that was protected better than the nuclear code. The six-billion-dollar trust currently benefited Marilyn and her two brothers and contained clauses that allowed the old man to control his kids from the grave. He rightly knew that bad marriages ruined lives—and fortunes—and had a clause inserted that carried a ten percent penalty for divorcing and a crippling fifty percent reduction if the required prenuptial agreement was violated.

Scaling Mount Kilimanjaro barefoot with a giraffe on my back would be easier than getting Marilyn to move off the mark.

"I . . . I guess we'll just keep things like they are."

She shook her head. "I'm afraid that's not going to be possible."

"What do you mean?"

"I'm going to file for divorce, Gideon. It's what we both want, and you'll have to leave the island."

Throat closing, I reached for the counter as Marilyn's voice began to fade. My mind scrambling amid the rising panic, I tried to recall the instructions my coach had told me. What was it? A doll, yes, make like a ragdoll, a limp ragdoll.

I slumped my head forward, sagged my shoulders and sucked in a deep abdominal breath. I held it for a count of five, releasing it slowly through my nose. As I began repeating the process, Marilyn's voice came into focus and I heard her say, "You're pathetic, you know that?"

Bile splashed against the rear of my throat. I'd hated her for years and thought endlessly about killing her. It was time to finally do it.

2

——————

BARNET WINES AND SPIRITS WAS SPREAD OVER THREE Waterside Shops storefronts. It was an unusual place for a liquor store, representing a gamble to offset the astronomical rent with sales of boutique wines and an entrée into serving the thriving charity scene in Naples. No expense was spared in building out the store's space. In a bid to rank with the philanthropic set, it featured a cave for private tastings and small events, along with luxurious retail space that looked like a world-class collector's cellar.

John Barnet closed the door to his office and sorted through the mail. A solid quarter of the stack were past-due notices, reinforcing the fact he'd placed his chips on the wrong horse. He pulled two of the oldest out and wrote checks dated a week ahead. Confident he'd find a way out, he pulled his six-foot six-inch frame out of his chair and headed to the bathroom to freshen up for his meeting.

Barnet was running a tiny comb through his Van Dyke when Marilyn knocked on the door. Wearing a white skirt and red blouse and dripping with jewelry, she immediately lifted Barnet's spirits.

"Mrs. Boggs. It's so nice to see you again."

He closed the door behind her and caressed her face. Pushing her pixie hair back, he hungrily kissed her. Marilyn returned the affection but pulled away when Barnet ran his hand up her skirt.

"Don't be such a bad boy, Johnny. This isn't the place."

Barnet smiled. "We still on tonight?"

Marilyn silently nodded and pouted her lips.

"I just got in a wonderful grower Champagne. It's highly allocated, but I know you'll love it. Nobody outside of New York's got it."

"Sounds special."

Barnet took her hand. "Not as special as you. I can't wait to see you later."

"Let's make it at the penthouse. I'm going to be downtown for a Leukemia Foundation meeting. Did you know I'm chairing the ball this year?"

"Very nice. Is it going to be at the Ritz again?"

She nodded.

"You know they don't allow outside beverage vendors."

"It's only one event, John."

"I know, but it is not fair. Besides, they serve second-rate plonk, and at crazy prices to boot. You know better than me, if you want folks to open their wallets you have to run a top-shelf event. I could put together something unique for you, maybe a nice mix of older Bordeaux and Napa cult wines that'll have people talking about the event a month later."

"You're probably right. I'll speak with them."

"You think they'll agree?"

She smiled. "Are you doubting me, Johnny?"

"Not in a zillion years, darling."

She looked at her watch. "I have a facial at two, so let's go over the St. Matthew House event."

"Sure."

Barnet pulled a file out and sat next to Marilyn, who said, "I hope you remembered that the majority of attendees aren't, shall we say, as sophisticated as usual."

"You forget I've been doing this for a while? Not to worry, I put together a nice selection, nothing over the top, that suits the crowd. Even the cheese selections are upper midrange."

"Sounds perfect. You've got the mimosa bar, right?"

"Yep. Though I think it would be a nice idea to add a tray of chocolates to every table."

"But the package from the Hyatt includes dessert."

"They're just going to give you a cheesy sheet cake. Having premium chocolates is a nice touch that they'll remember." He snapped his fingers. "It just hit me; what about giving every attendee a little box, nothing big, say a selection of four chocolates?"

"I like it, but I don't want to give the impression that we're spending too much money on the affair."

"Leave it to me. I'll have the boxes printed with something like, 'Courtesy of the Boggs Foundation,' or something like that."

"I like that idea. How much do you think it will run?"

"Asking prices? What, are you on a budget all of a sudden?"

"Of course not, just curious."

"Don't worry, I'll work it out for you."

"Thanks, Johnny. I've got to get moving."

"By any chance did you bring a check with you? I don't want to give my people the impression I'm not following company procedure."

. . .

NODDING, Marilyn pulled a matching Hermes checkbook out of her pocketbook. "How much you need?"

"Uh, let's make it an even fifteen thousand."

MARILYN'S PERFUME was still in the air when he summoned his store manager into his office.

"What's up, John?"

Barnet held out Marilyn's check. "Run this right over to the bank."

"No problem."

Bridgette took the check but didn't leave.

Barnet said, "That's all I needed."

"Can I ask you something?"

"Sure."

"It's personal, but I don't have a brother or anyone to ask about it."

"It's okay, what's going on?"

"Well, there's this guy, Gary, and he won't leave me alone. He's always coming by my place and he makes me uncomfortable."

"Were you involved with this guy?"

"No, never. He creeps me out. He's like stalking me. And I don't know what to do about it. What should I do?"

Barnet leaned back in his chair. "Back in L.A., we had this preacher type guy who used to hang around in front of my Cienega Boulevard store. He'd try to tell the winos to stop drinking and just kept interfering with the customers. I told him to stop, but he'd be there rain or shine, and it started to hurt sales."

"Wow, what did you do?"

"He'd park in Randy's Donuts lot, and one night I waited in the dark for him and he never came back again."

"What'd you tell him to get him to stop?"

"There wasn't much talking, but I hear he spent a couple of weeks in ICU."

3

BARNET HAD BEEN TO THE FIFTH AVENUE penthouse a couple of dozen times. He parked below the building, putting his white Porsche next to Marilyn's baby-blue Bentley. The garage was nicer than his first place in Los Angeles, but, as the elevator door shut, he couldn't help thinking that the prices these places commanded were ridiculous. He checked his hair in the chrome doors' reflection just before the doors opened into her spacious apartment.

Greeted by Simon and Garfunkel crooning at full volume, Barnet made a beeline to the kitchen's audio console and lowered it. As usual, Marilyn was never ready on time. He knew she used every opportunity to prove she was better than the rest of the world. She had it too damn easy, he thought. Never worked a day in her life. Marilyn was spoon-fed all right, and it was a platinum one, not silver.

She didn't understand how lucky she was, Barnet thought, surveying the penthouse of seven thousand square feet that was a 180 from Keewaydin Island. The designer here used an edgy combination of Miami, New York, and Los Angeles styling that made you feel like you didn't know where you were. Barnet liked the feel of the place and loved that he could head downstairs and roam along Fifth when he hit his limit of Marilyn.

He took a glass ice bucket from a sleek cabinet in the bar, put the Champagne in and filled it with ice. Grabbing a bottle of Aubert Chardonnay out of the cooler, he reminded himself that the weekly rendezvous was vital to keeping things together. Noting the wine was from the Ritchie vineyard, Barnet pulled the cork. After a deep sniff and a sip, he poured a healthy glass.

A light buzz is what he needed to get through the night. Sipping his wine, he circled the room, appreciating the contemporary art that graced its walls. He wondered how much they were worth, marveling at how perfectly they fit the place. He tipped back the remains of a second glass as Marilyn made her entrance.

"Starting without me?"

Barnet put an arm around her and kissed her.

"Let me pop the Champagne. This is something special. You're gonna like it."

"What is it?"

As he took the foil and cage off the cork, he said, "Le Mont Benoit Extra Brut. It's what is known as a grower Champagne. Emmanuel Brochet is the producer and the grower, and their Champagnes are made only with grapes from his vineyard. Most Champagnes, like Moet and even Dom Perignon, buy grapes from across the region and blend them. They also blend Champagnes from different vintages to make a Champagne that fits the style they're known for. The growers don't do that; they make Champagnes that represent the property and the weather of that year."

"They're more expensive?"

He popped the cork, saying, "Sometimes, and they should

be. I mean, if the weather is bad, they have it all on the line. It's risky, and I like that commitment. Here, try some."

"It's good."

"Can you tell how fresh it is? It's amazing."

"I think so."

"Brochet is a genius, and the place is totally organic."

"That's good. Maybe we should get a winery."

"That'd be nice, but you can't do it in Florida."

"Why not?"

"The climate. Anyway, what's for dinner?"

"Gemma made rosemary chicken and grilled vegetables for us."

AFTER DINNER BARNET pulled the cork out of a Biondi Santi Brunello and poured a glass.

"You want some?"

"Not now, I can't keep up with you."

"It's one I procured for you." He held up the glass. "And it's lovely."

"I'm glad you're enjoying it."

"I gotta say, I just love the artwork here. Especially that pink one."

"That's by a German artist. I can't remember his name. I think it's Richter or something."

"Where'd you find that?"

"Gideon picked it up at a Sotheby's auction."

"Real nice one. Did he get the others as well?"

"Yeah, all of them. He's really into his art."

"He did an amazing job. I wouldn't have bought any of them, if I had the money to spend on art, but they work so well here."

"It's the only thing he's good at these days."

"Well, he got it right."

"Gideon said he wants a divorce."

"So? Why not?"

"The trust will reduce my benefits if I divorce."

"Wow. So, Daddy's still calling the shots while the grass grows over him."

"I know it's crazy, but what can I do? I want to get away from him, but it's going to cost me."

"Maybe Gideon could disappear."

"What? What are you saying, John?"

"Just that. If he were to disappear, you'd be free from him and you wouldn't take the hit. That's a nice solution, don't you think?"

4

GIDEON BRIGHTHOUSE

THE MORE I THOUGHT ABOUT IT, THE MORE THE IDEA GREW, like a weed. I had to find a plausible way to kill Marilyn, one that wouldn't implicate me. There, I said it, and it didn't feel bad. It really wasn't my fault; she's the one who's forcing me. I don't really have a choice.

If there was another way out of this marriage that allowed me to stay on the island, I'd grab it in a heartbeat. It's not the money, it's really not. Naturally, people would think that, but they'd be wrong. Most people don't understand what someone like me has to endure. The panic is crippling. Nothing gets through. You could shoot a gun next to my ear and I'd still hear nothing but the blood pounding in my head. I can only imagine what they say when it overwhelms me.

Whatever method I decide on, it can't be violent, nothing like shooting her, unless I can set it up to look like a robbery. She has massive amounts of jewelry and was careless, make that stupid, about it. Bottom line was she lost things all the time, or maybe her boyfriend stole some of her things when they got together. Except for a piece or two her daddy got her,

Marilyn didn't care if something got lost or was stolen; she'd just replace it.

What if it looked like a drug-crazed addict had broken in? They're everywhere, but they'd need a boat to get here. What if it happened in town? But how would I accomplish that? Forget that idea. I picked up the da Vinci biography I had been reading.

A huge formation of gray clouds rushed in from the south, darkening things as the wind picked up. I kept reading until I felt a drop and headed inside the pool house as the sky opened up. The TV was blaring nonsense from one of those ridiculous reality court shows and I flicked the remote, landing on an episode of *American Crime Story*.

I stood, book in hand, watching as a husband said he'd gotten away with killing his wife. The guy looked like an average Joe and spoke like he'd barely finished high school. The show shifted to an image of a smoldering site, the sole hint it had been a house being the brick chimney was still standing. I inched closer to the screen as an actor reenacted the crime.

The actress playing the wife left the house during the afternoon, and her estranged husband slipped in and went to the den where she watched television each night. He explained that the lamp he was standing before went on automatically each night at eleven as a security light. He removed the bulb from the lamp, pocketed it, and replaced it with one of a dramatically higher wattage. The narrator explained that the lamp was rated for a maximum 100 watts, and that the husband had replaced it with a 200-watt bulb.

Bulb replaced, the husband took a couple of tissues from the bathroom and laid them over the new bulb, ensuring that if the inappropriate bulb didn't cause a fire that the heat would ignite the tissues as his wife slept. I couldn't believe it

5

BARNET SAT AT HIS DESK WATCHING CAMERA FEEDS OF THE floor of his store. The intermittent, drip-like foot traffic troubled him. Dragging himself off his chair, he walked out of his office and began circling the empty store. Forcing a smile at the four sales associates who were chatting, he made himself a promise to cut staff down to two as summer approached.

The reality of a further slowing as the season wound down, forced Barnet to retreat to his office again. Maybe it was time to focus on Internet sales. Online competitors were biting into his sales, and going on the offense would bring orders in. He thought the idea of putting together a campaign highlighting his unusual store had merit.

Logging on to Winesearch.com he scanned rows of offers. How the hell were these guys making any money? The margins he saw were minuscule. Barnet believed the business was about suggestions, introducing and convincing clients to experience new regions and varietals. Staying away from the commodity side of things sold in huge numbers by big players was not only far more interesting, it provided a chance to make a decent return on each bottle.

He walked over to the fridge and grabbed a bottle of Red Juice Press. As he twisted the cap off, he spied an empty bottle of Chateau Margaux from 2000. Recalling the dark-blue and red fruit present in the trophy wine, it hit him. He took a guzzle of juice and pressed the intercom button.

"Bridgette, can I see you for a moment?"

Before he finished another swallow of the deep-red drink, the store's general manager came in.

"What's up?"

Barnet was disgusted at the roll of fat around her waist. "Sit. I'd like to make a real push into the futures business."

"Bordeaux, right?"

"Naturally. It'll help us ride out the summer."

"It's a good idea. There's a lot of collectors down here, and if we do it right, we'll grab a nice slice of the market."

"As far as I know, Jacques from Bleu Provence has the strongest futures program, but you've been down here a lot longer than I have."

She nodded. "Yeah, Bleu Cellar has been at it for a while, and they have most of the Port Royal buyers."

"Thought so. Look, you know me, I never want to give anything away, but for this, let's position our prices under all the major players. At this point, it's about working our way into the collector market, and the cash flow won't hurt either."

"We've got a decent email list we can market off of."

"That's a great tool. We should have a couple of banners made for the store, and I'd like to do some Facebook ads targeting wine drinkers and especially Francophiles. Also, we'll do a couple of ads in the *Daily News*."

"It's a good idea, but are we going be able to get Margaux, Haut-Brion, and Petrus?"

Barnet nodded. "Why wouldn't we?"

"We had a . . . uh . . . an issue last year, if you remember."

"Everything got settled, but if they don't want to play ball, screw 'em. We don't need them anyway."

"I don't know about that, John. We've got to be careful. Many buyers place all their futures with the same retailer."

Barnet knew not having those wineries would eliminate a fat slice of potential buyers, but said, "How quickly can you get a campaign together?"

"Fast. Graphics aren't an issue. Say, within a week. But we'll need to nail down the producers and what we're going to price things at."

"Find out what Bleu Cellar, ABC, and Total Wine are selling at and come in five percent below the lowest of them."

"That will get some attention for sure, but I really need to know about Margaux, Brion, and Petrus. Are you going to see if they'll sell to us this season?"

"Assume they will. If they give us any hassles, I'll wave the pile of orders we get at them."

"Are you sure?"

"One hundred percent. Now, get cracking."

Barnet knew the storied wineries would never sell to him, but he needed the cash flow the futures would provide. The eighteen months until the wine would arrive would give him time to explore other ways to increase sales and reduce costs. As for any disgruntled futures buyers, he'd deal with them when the time came.

LEAVING HIS STORE, Barnet made a left, past the dancing fountains and lululemon and into the corridor that housed the offices of the Forbes Company. He knew the meeting with the owners of Waterside Shops would be difficult. Before opening the gold-lettered door, he reminded himself to curb his pride.

The management offices were perfunctory, providing a stark contrast with the opulent feel of the outdoor mall. He stood waiting until Albert Chesny, the managing director, was ready.

In keeping with providing as much retail space as possible, Chesny's office was smaller than the size of most Port Royal kitchen islands.

They shook hands over a steel desk piled with files.

"It's good to see you, John."

"Same here, Al."

"Hey, thanks for that recommendation you gave me on that cabernet."

"My pleasure, I'm glad you liked it. We've got a couple of nice new ones from Washington State you should try."

"My wife's throwing a dinner party next week. I'll stop in and pick up a few bottles."

"I can take care of it for you. It's what we do at Barnet's."

"Thanks, but we're keeping it low-key, so nothing fancy. What can I do for you?"

Barnet shifted in his chair. "Things are really slowing down early this year. I'm sure everybody in here feels the drop-off."

"Actually, foot traffic is up almost six and a half percent this month."

"Really? Everyone in town seems to be complaining."

"We don't focus on the rest of town, John. Waterside is a unique shopping experience."

"It's special, that's why I took the chance in locating my store here."

"And we appreciate the vote of confidence. You made the right decision."

"I hope so. It's an unusual location for a beverage store."

Chesny said, "Barnet's is more than a beverage store. You're selling an experience. That's why we were excited to have you as part of the Waterside family."

"I still believe Waterside has the right traffic and cachet we need, but I'm not going to beat around the bush, Al; the operating costs are sky-high."

"We believe our pricing structure is commensurate with the exposure and traffic our tenants receive. You know we're the best game in town, John."

"I'm not disputing the uniqueness of Waterside, but it's taking us more time to build our business. I'd like you to consider a reduction in our rent. It would be temporary, just to get us over the hump."

Chesny shook his head. "I'm sorry, but we're unable to accommodate your request, John."

Barnet leaned forward. "We could really use a little help here, Al. You know what the summer is like."

"I'm sure you understand that it's not that easy to adjust leases. I understand your situation and have an idea I can probably get everyone on board with."

Barnet moved to the edge of his seat. "I really appreciate your help here."

"Presently, you occupy three southern storefronts. Why don't you give some consideration to giving one or even two stores back to us? I'm sure we'd be able to work a waiver for altering the lease, and you could cut your expenses by a third or even two-thirds."

Barnet fell back in his chair. "I can't do that. It'd be the kiss of death."

"Rightsizing is smart, John. I think you should give it some thought."

6

GIDEON BRIGHTHOUSE

I SQUEEZED MY EYES SHUT, GENTLY MASSAGING MY EYEBALLS and brows before returning to the screen. A couple of interesting ideas had surfaced during the three hours of hunting, giving me plenty to debate. The most intriguing concept involved a poisonous fish. It was crazy that people would even consider eating a blowfish, but to the Japanese it was a delicacy. Marilyn enjoyed sushi, so plausibly she would try it, especially since it was so expensive and came with bragging rights.

A bunch of deaths, mainly in Japan, occurred each year from the poison in blowfish. It sounded perfect, because unless you had a highly qualified chef who knew how to properly fillet a blowfish, you'd die. It only took a tiny bit of the poison to kill a human, and there wasn't a known antidote. Death comes quickly via respiratory failure. I shook out of my head an image of Marilyn gasping, and resumed my research.

A Google search of Japanese restaurants populated a small list. Most were the Thai sushi places that dotted Naples, but none of them offered blowfish. There wasn't a place in either Collier or Lee County that did. The closest was in Miami, and that wouldn't work. Maybe there was a way for cross contamination. Boy that would throw the police off.

Noting the poison in a blowfish was tetrodotoxin, I continued researching and found that blue-ringed octopuses also contained it. Marilyn ate grilled octopus all the time; said it was super low in calories and had a lot of nutrients in it. Wouldn't that be ironic?

I typed "deadly poison" into the search bar and was surprised by the long list that appeared. Polonium? What the heck is that? It's 250,000 times deadlier than hydrogen cyanide? I pulled my hands away from the keyboard. It's some radioactive substance. The next couple were gases that needed to be inhaled, making them unacceptable. What about this hydrogen cyanide? Oh, it's another gas.

Here's the blowfish poison again. It was good to see it ranking sixth on the list, but I already knew it was a good one. Then there was amatoxin, a poison found in mushrooms. It sounded perfect and I envisioned slipping the mushrooms into her juicer. After she ingested it, Marilyn would become dizzy, short of breath, and have a headache. Then her liver and kidneys would shut down and she'd lapse into a coma, dying a few days later. Originally, I believed I was looking for something immediate. But as I rolled it around, taking a few days, the coma, organs shutting down, I realized it provided some cover.

When someone dies unexpectedly, everyone starts asking questions, and that's dangerous. If Marilyn experienced symptoms and lingered a few days, things would cloud up. It would be interesting to discover if the poison would dissipate as she was in a coma. It normally did, didn't it? Her body would still be functioning, processing the poison. It would provide a measure of camouflage in case of an autopsy. I sat back—this could be it.

I READ IT AGAIN. How could it be this easy? Everything you needed to know about killing someone was available with a Google search. This was dangerous. And there was all kinds of information about how to hide the fact you did it. I did another search and stared at the screen in shock. I counted: there were eleven sources to buy the poisonous mushrooms.

The first listing was Xiamen Enterprises, and they had a bazaar-like website offering an eBay assortment of swag items for sale. The last thing I needed was fake poison, so I bounced off and scrolled halfway down to a link for the innocuous-sounding Beatrice Solutions. A skimpy web page in Russian popped up. I hit the British flag icon and it converted the text to English. The headline touted their confidentiality and featured a picture of Edward Snowden. They offered a long list of chemicals for sale, and I hunted through them.

Bingo. They offered amatoxin by the tenth of a milligram at five hundred dollars per tenth. That seemed expensive. Opening another window, I checked the lethal amount I needed, which was .7 milligrams. That's tiny—the smallest pill I took for my anxiety was 10 mg, and this was fifteen times smaller. Could that be all that was needed?

7

GIDEON BRIGHTHOUSE

It was a bit past five when I headed for a walk on the beach. It was one of my favorite times of the day; the sun was hanging halfway up and its intensity had dwindled. I watched a pair of pelicans glide just offshore, studying the glistening water for dinner opportunities. One of them suddenly swooped down and dove below the surface. After it resurfaced, I began thinking the entire situation through.

I had to be rock-certain sure there was no other way. As much as I despised Marilyn, killing her was considerably outside the norm. You need advice on contemporary art? I'm your counselor. Political advice? Well, Florida's Democratic Party used to call me their go-to guy, but that was before Senator White was defeated by a virtual unknown.

But that wasn't my fault, and the media missed the fact that a revolution was taking place. People were tired of the same old faces who talked great plans but were so self-interested that nothing ever got done. White never had a chance, not that he deserved it. After two terms, he didn't even have one piece of legislation to call his own. A dozen years of so-called public service and he never even sponsored a parking ordinance. Then came the pay-for-play charges, and both of our careers were over.

To be honest, I didn't miss it, but Marilyn sure did. She relished being close to the powerful, and if there was a power center in America, Washington, DC was it. Her family's profile was already elevated, so the combo we formed as a couple opened a lot of doors, and we were invited to numerous events at the White House. The family spread its money around, and that kept Marilyn in the social scene for a while after White lost, but the winds were blowing against the financial industry, and politicians avoided their donors in public.

It was tough to accept that she'd been so superficial, but looking back there didn't seem to be any doubt. When I suffered the heart attack a week after the new senator was sworn in, Marilyn rallied, staying overnight with me at NCH. I had four blockages that were serious, and Marilyn demanded that the head of cardiology be brought in for the angioplasty.

The physical recovery was quick, but I was a mental mess. The doctors said that depression was common with heart attacks. I was not only down but scared out of my mind. I don't know why, but I was suddenly afraid of being with people, especially in crowded places. Receiving visitors at the hospital and then at the Port Royal home made me sweat. It was impossible to talk, other than to parrot that I was feeling okay.

The anxiety I was experiencing subsided dramatically when we decamped to Keewaydin Island. When I explained to Marilyn that I was feeling peaceful because of Keewaydin, she dismissed it, saying it was the medication that made me relaxed. Her theory was tested less than two weeks later when we flew to Boston for a shareholder meeting.

Attending the annual meeting was another requirement that her father had dictated into the trust, so into the boat we had climbed. Once off the mainland, we got into a car with heavily tinted windows, and as soon as the door closed I felt the need to open a window.

"Close the window, Gideon," Marilyn said.

"I need to get some air."

"The air conditioning is on. Close it before the wind ruins my hair."

I raised the window with one hand and adjusted the vent with the other, directing the airflow at my face. As I leaned forward, Marilyn said, "What's the matter now?"

"I don't know. Just felt a little something; maybe I'm just a little hot."

I closed my eyes, begging myself to settle down.

Ten minutes later we swung into Naples Airport and made our way to the hanger where our Flexjet plane was waiting. The silver Learjet had its stairway down, and as we walked over to board I said, "This jet seems smaller than usual."

"I guess Robert arranged it since it's only the two of us."

I had to bend down to pass through the door, and as soon as I did, my heart raced and I froze for a second before backing out onto the stairs. I tried to control my panting as Marilyn said, "Gideon! What the hell is going on?"

"Uh, hold on a minute."

"Get on! We're taking off."

"Give me a minute."

"Hurry up, damn it! We're running tight as it is."

I took three deep breaths, and eyes on my feet, shuffled on board. I fumbled in my bag for headphones as I eased into a seat.

"Are you all right?"

"Yeah, just a little claustrophobic."

"What? Now you're claustrophobic?"

"I don't know what's happening, Marilyn. It just came on, out of nowhere."

"You're pathetic."

How could she say something like that? "You're cruel, you know that?"

Marilyn sighed heavily and went back to her *Cosmopolitan* magazine as the cabin door closed. Eyes shut, I concentrated on trying to hear each individual violin playing Vivaldi's *Four Seasons*, but as we sat waiting for clearance, fear crept up my belly into my throat. I was about to rip off my seat belt when the jet lurched forward and we headed toward the runway. My anxiety lessened as the engine roar got louder. It wasn't until I was pushed back into my seat by the g-force that I opened my eyes.

After landing, a tightness in my chest sprouted as we climbed the stairs into the gate area. My "excuse mes" got harsher as we weaved our way to Logan's pick-up area. Though it was dark and depressing, it felt good to get outside and into a waiting car. Two minutes later, Marilyn got in the car, saying, "I don't know what's going on with you, Gideon, but you've got to calm down."

"I'm fine."

"Really? You ran through the terminal like it was on fire."

"I—I needed some air."

"You need to get this under control, and fast. You better not embarrass me tonight."

"Don't worry, I'll be okay tonight and tomorrow."

"Tomorrow you can stay at the hotel. Say you're sick or whatever, but you know tonight is important."

I might take her up on it. Tomorrow would be a zoo, with hundreds of shareholders and gobs of media all day long. And boy, was it a long day. Tonight's soiree at the Intercontinental was for the family, a couple of major shareholders, and the trustees who oversaw the Boggs trust, which controlled a good hunk of the company stock. It amounted to a chance for the family to do a pulse check on each other and was another one of the old man's ways of keeping an eye on things from the cemetery.

I understood what he tried to do, and maybe I would do the same but for a couple of things, like not allowing my wife to adopt my last name, which was silly. Even the generally accepted combo of Boggs and Brighthouse was prohibited, unless you wanted to forgo some income, and Marilyn said it was silly to be penalized. I should have fought that and a lot of other so-called guidelines and maybe we wouldn't be where we were today.

Originally, I chalked it up to wealth and a certain quirkiness, until I lost a good friend.

I was in my office when Mark Simone came in, and I jumped to my feet.

"Hey Mark. What a pleasant surprise." I came around my desk and extended a hand that was left hanging.

Mark Simone, who worked for the *Sentinel*, slumped into a chair. "They're fucking monsters."

"Who? What's going on, Mark?"

"Like you don't know."

"I have no idea what you're referring to."

"I got canned because of your wife's fucking family."

My stomach dropped. "What happened?"

"You know I was writing that series on the mutual fund industry."

"Sure."

"Well, God forbid I mentioned that brush with the SEC."

"Over the marketing materials?"

"Yeah."

"But that was settled without a fine or any repercussions."

"I know; it was nothing. All I was trying to do was show how regulated things were, that's all. I wasn't taking a swipe at the Boggs."

"Of course, but what happened?"

"Next thing I know my editor is all over me about mentioning the Boggs family, even though he was the one who approved the article. He was covering up, and next thing I know HR calls me in and I got the boot."

"Are you sure it was over that?"

"We've known each other a long time. Trust me, that's what happened."

"Let me see what I can do."

"Man, you know how ignorant you sound? You think you're gonna get them to reverse it?"

"But if that is why they did it, it's unfair and baseless."

Mark shook his head. "*If* they did it? Man, you're blind, buddy."

As soon as Mark left, I called the family office. I can still hear Peter Gerey tell me it was a family matter and not up for discussion. It took me two weeks to get the nerve to tell Mark I was unable to influence the situation. He hung up on me and had refused to take any of my calls since then.

THE BOGGS WERE PRESBYTERIAN, but they felt more like Mormons. A set percentage was donated to charity, and they required their children to perform two years of community service before working for the firm. Marilyn did her service with St. Matthew's House in Naples but never really worked for the family firm. She said she wasn't interested in business and preferred to help others, but shortly after we met I realized she didn't feel smart enough. Her brothers had MBAs from Harvard and were sharp, if condescending. When we first met, the vibe was clear they didn't respect me, but I momentarily turned things around when the art that I recommended they purchase ran up in value.

What it came down to was they were all phony. I often wondered if Marilyn was worse than her brothers or if they were all the same, but I knew Marilyn better and hated her more. I was certain she didn't breathe a word of our relationship difficulties to anyone in the family and equally certain I'd be persona non grata, and thrown off the island as well, if the news leaked.

HAVING TAKEN AN EXTRA VALIUM, I believed another attempt to discuss things with Marilyn had good prospects. She was sitting on the deck with her morning coffee and flinched when I slid the door open.

"Sorry."

"Damn you, Gideon. I almost spilled my coffee. What do you want now?"

"I was hoping we could discuss an amicable way to end our marriage."

"There's no need, the prenuptial dictates everything."

"I understand that, but I know going that route would have negative financial consequences for you. Can't we find another solution?"

She set her cup down and smiled. "There is another solution."

I pulled a chair out and was about to sit. "That's great. What is it?"

"You don't want to know."

"Of course, I do."

She looked me straight in the eye. "John suggested he could have you disappear. That would take care of things, wouldn't it?"

I grabbed the back of the chair. "What? What is that supposed to mean?"

"Take it any way you want. But since you're an invalid, I'll decide what happens."

Right there and then I decided Marilyn had to go before they killed me. As soon as I got back to the house I'd order the mushroom poison.

8

———

A KNOCK ON HIS OFFICE DOOR PROMPTED BARNET TO CHECK the video monitor. He smiled when the camera feed revealed it was Marilyn. He'd dodged her calls for three straight days and her showing up played right into his hands. He buzzed her in and rose to greet her.

"Marilyn. I didn't expect you."

"You didn't call me back. I was getting worried about you."

Barnet kissed her but avoided hugging her.

"I'm all right, just working twenty-four seven, trying to keep this place together."

"Why? What's the matter?"

"Oh, forget it. You don't want to know."

"Of course I want to know. What's going on?"

"Don't worry about it. I'll figure it out."

"Figure what out? Tell me what's going on, John."

Barnet flopped into his chair. "The off-season is killing us. I don't know why this time around things are so bad, but they are."

"It'll turn around, it always does."

Barnet shrugged. "Maybe."

"What are you so down about?"

"I don't want to drag you into all this."

"It's okay, really. I want to be involved. Maybe I can help somehow."

"Well, you know we made a big push for the futures, and we're getting sales, but I've got to front half the money for all these orders, and on top of that I sunk a ton of money into the catering side of things, and that didn't exactly work out like I planned."

"I thought the catering idea you had was good. You just have to give it time."

Barnet exhaled dejectedly. "Time, I don't have. These bastards here had the gall to serve a pre-default notice on me. Can you believe it?"

"Default? Can they do that?"

Barnet threw his hands up. "And we're only two weeks behind on the rent. It's crazy."

"How much is due?"

"Forty thousand."

"Really? Forty thousand? That's expensive."

"Tell me about it."

"I could help some."

"Really? I don't want to involve you, Marilyn, but I really don't know what to do. If you could help, that'd be incredibly generous of you."

"You know I'd be happy to help you, John. I'll lend you ten thousand."

"Oh, that'll help a little."

BEFORE SITTING BEHIND HIS DESK, Barnet guzzled two bottles of water, attempting to curb a light hangover. He set another bottle on his desk and looked over yesterday's receipts. Flinging the tally to the side, he opened a red file labeled Futures.

After scanning the two pages in it, Barnet got up and yanked his office door open.

"Bridgette! Where's Bridgette? I need her. Now!"

He slammed the door and paced the room for a minute until there was a knock on the door.

"Come in!"

"Hey, John, you needed something?"

"What the hell's going on with the futures?"

"What do you mean?"

He grabbed the file and waved it.

"This. This is what I mean. It's a joke."

Bridgette glanced at the file. "I'm sorry, but I don't understand."

"Is this all the orders?"

"Yes. Unless something came in this morning."

"Are you telling me twenty measly orders is all we have?"

"There's a lot of competition out there, John. Besides, a lot of people are out of town this time of the year."

"You ever hear of the phone? We can take a damn order over the phone!"

"We've, we've been talking and emailing our targets. We're really not doing that bad, John."

"Are you kidding me? You know how much it's costing me to advertise? What's the damn point of this?"

"I—I—"

"Get back out there and sell some damn wine! I've got a lot to do."

. . .

BARNET FLOPPED onto his sofa and had just closed his eyes when his cell rang. He yanked it from his pocket. It was Marilyn. He swiped the call away, put his feet on the coffee table and began rummaging through a bank of ideas he had accumulated to keep the store afloat. After twenty minutes of soul-searching, he got up, opened his laptop, went to Amazon's site, and began browsing.

9

Four days later, Marilyn closed the door to Barnet's office and said, "How could you do this to me?"

"It was a mistake, that's all."

"I'm so embarrassed, I don't know what to do."

"You shouldn't be. It was nothing, just a simple miscalculation."

Marilyn put her hands on her hips. "My reputation is on the line, John."

"That's crazy. With your money, what do they think you're doing, stealing?"

"Of course not. But they'll think I'm incompetent, and that's worse than stealing. The philanthropic community is built on trust. Our donors rely on us to be good shepherds of their money. Any rumors or even a whiff of impropriety, intentional or not, and they'll go running."

"Would you stop being an alarmist already?"

"It's easy for you to say that, but this is my life, John."

"What? Are you saying I don't care about you? That's crazy."

"I know, but John, this really makes me look bad. It's a lot of money, and I'm sure people are talking about it."

"I'll make sure Bridgette cuts a check today."

"I already reimbursed St. Vincent de Paul."

"You did? You ask me, I think you should have waited."

"I had to resolve it immediately."

"I understand, but I don't like the way it looks."

"What do you mean?"

"Look at it this way, you reimbursed the overcharge before going to the vendor. It could look a little fishy."

"Oh no, you think so?"

"Don't get nuts, Marilyn. I'm just thinking out loud."

"You see, you see how this could all be misinterpreted?"

"It won't be. They got their money back, and you have your story to tell about an overcharge."

"Story?"

"Come on, Marilyn, you know what I mean." Barnet got up and headed to the wine cooler. "Take it easy. Everything's going to be fine. Let's have a glass of white Burgundy. I just got in this delicious Burg from Domaine Leroy. You're gonna love it."

THE FOLLOWING morning Barnet was catching the sun on a bench outside his store. He greeted the UPS man, who was wheeling a stack of boxes into his store. A couple of minutes later, the store manager stepped outside holding a small box.

"This has your name on it, John. Is it for the store?"

Barnet took the Amazon package. "No, it's mine. I ordered a new external hard drive."

"Good idea. I need to back up my laptop. I don't trust this cloud thing."

"Me neither. Those guys are going to get hacked like everybody else."

"Only a matter of time. I gotta go. The Southern Wine truck is out back with a delivery."

Barnet took ten more minutes of sun before going back into the store. He went straight to his office and locked the door. He eased his tall frame into a chair and opened the package. Fingering the tiny device, Barnet marveled at how much smaller it was than the one he'd used before. He slipped the thumb-sized unit and charging cord into his breast pocket and threw the packing materials, after tearing them into small pieces, into the trash.

Stroking his Van Dyke, Barnet ran through his idea to buy time again. Satisfied there were no holes in it, he decided the sooner the better. It was Friday and he'd see Marilyn later, as usual. Tonight would be the night.

10

Marilyn nuzzled up to Barnet, snaking her hand down his thighs. When Barnet didn't react, she straightened up.

"What's the matter, John?"

"I don't know, not feeling up to it I guess."

"Did you drink too much again?"

"No, it's the first bottle."

She got off the couch. "Oh, well, maybe we just need to open another then."

"Or maybe we just need a little excitement to get things going, you know, a little kickoff help."

"I certainly hope you're not talking about any kind of drugs, John. You know I don't engage in those types of activities."

"No way; you know the only drug for me is wine."

"Then what are you talking about?"

"It's nothing to get crazy about. So, don't get mad or anything."

Marilyn crossed her arms. "I don't like the sound of this, John."

"Forget it then."

"Now that you brought it up, you've got to tell me."

"Well, I just thought, you know, something to start a little spark to get me going."

"I'm offended you need more than me to get things going, John. Frankly, it's hurtful."

"That's the point, it's nothing more than you."

Marilyn sat down next to John and ran her hand through his curly hair. "That's so sweet of you. So, what, inspiration shall we say, are you referring to?"

John reached into his rear pocket and pulled his phone out. Holding it horizontally, he hit play and a video jumped to life. When Marilyn saw herself naked with her ankles in the air, she screamed, "Oh my God! What have you done?"

"It's nothing, just—"

Marilyn jumped off the couch. "Nothing? That's me. We . . . we . . . that's personal. How could you do that to me?"

"I was only—"

"Only what? You filmed me without my permission!"

Barnet shrugged. "I knew you'd say no."

"So, you went ahead anyway? And I'm supposed to be fine with that?"

"I thought you'd appreciate it, sort of a memento. I think our time together is special."

"It was; now I'm not so sure."

"Come on, Marilyn you're making too big a thing about this. Everybody does it."

"I thought you knew Marilyn Boggs is not just anybody."

"I do. You're very special to me."

"I want that video, John, and I want it now. It's got to be deleted. If that ever gets into the wrong hands I'd be destroyed, and the family would be disgraced."

"Okay, okay, I get it. Look, I'll delete it now if it makes you feel better."

"Yes, it would."

"You sure you don't want to see the whole thing? There's a really good part a little further on."

"What's wrong with you, John Barnet? Destroy the damn thing now or it's over between us."

"All right already. I just thought . . . but, forget it. It wasn't such a good idea, I guess."

"It's totally offensive. I can't believe you did it."

"I'm sorry, really, I was just trying to, I don't know, I thought it might be fun."

"Fun? Are you losing your mind, John?"

He hung his head. "Believe me, I didn't mean to upset you, Marilyn. It was a mistake. I see that now, and I apologize for doing it." Barnet took the phone and hit delete. "It's gone now. Can you forgive me?"

11

GIDEON BRIGHTHOUSE

I came in from a long walk on the beach. It was so peaceful, I'd forgotten about how hot it was. A swim in the pool would be perfect. I decided to grab a towel and take a dip.

Sliding a door open, I saw a package on my desk and perked up. The Jasper Johns notebooks I purchased from the Sotheby's auction had arrived. It was wonderful to be able to submit your bids online and not have to deal with going in person.

Approaching the desk, I could see the Sotheby package, but what was the other parcel? Picking up the package, it felt empty. I grabbed a pair of scissors and cut the top off the plastic envelope. Inside was a harder plastic enclosure. When I saw the Russian lettering, I dropped the package and scanned the area.

Shivering with the realization the mushrooms had arrived, I began pacing the room. Keeping this in the closet as I had planned didn't feel right anymore. Could it be toxic, just breathing around it? Could you even trust the Russians to package it correctly? They probably didn't care. I'd have to

Google if these mushrooms emit fumes that are harmful. Was it even safe to touch without gloves?

What the heck did I get myself involved in? I should just discard them before it's too late. Oh man, what was I thinking? No way I can go through with this. Inhaling deeply, I told myself to calm down. I was about to plop on the sofa when I realized I was sweaty and headed up for a shower.

Halfway up the stairs, I made a U-turn and came down. Grabbing a dish towel from the kitchen, I wrapped the mushroom package in it. After slipping it in the cabinet beneath the cooktop, I went back up the stairs.

While showering, I thought through a bunch of hiding places. I needed somewhere the housekeepers wouldn't find it. Keeping it outside the house made sense, but I couldn't risk the maintenance crew uncovering it.

Every place I considered had flaws. Toweling off, I mentally rummaged through idea after idea, rejecting them all as I got dressed and went downstairs.

Sitting at the kitchen table, I remembered this TV show where a killer had kept poison in his kitchen's spice rack. It was nervy, but I liked it and settled on keeping it in plain sight when a delivery man knocked and slid open a door. He was carrying the pool house's weekly floral arrangement.

He placed a large triangular vase overflowing with massive stems of birds of paradise and left. Admiring how the orange flowers contrasted with the black vase, an idea hit me and I went to the art house.

Flicking on the lights, the building came alive, highlighting its special lighting. I loved this place. How many nights did I sleep in here before the right mix of meds contained my anxiety? Even after things settled down, I'd considered moving in here, but it wasn't practical. With only a half bath and no kitchen, it would needlessly complicate life, something I needed less than most people.

There were plenty of spots to hide the slim package. It could be taped under one of the viewing benches, secured behind a painting, or even dropped inside a sculpture. Besides the odd appraiser or insurance representative, no one came in here but me. It was perfect.

Circling the room, I thought the best place would be to tape it to the underside of one of the velour benches, whose pale green fabric had a couple of inches of overhang. The cleaning girls would never see it. I settled on a bench that faced a Richard Prince piece called *Even Lower Manhattan*. Dark in both its color red and mood, Prince had inserted an unreadable piece of newsprint by the edge of the painting. The mystery of the piece drew me in every time. I wanted to reach into the painting, pull the newspaper out, and read what it was about.

The air conditioning kicked on, breaking my concentration. I'd have to wait until the staff left to hide it.

WHERE'S THE TAPE? I needed the heavy kind. Couldn't trust scotch tape with this, and I couldn't ask the maintenance guys. After checking all the kitchen drawers, I headed to my desk. Sitting on top of the desk was a box from Microsoft. My new laptop had finally arrived. Tugging at the tape, I opened the box but took a layer of cardboard with it. I froze. No way I wanted that to happen with the mushroom packaging; I could poison myself. If I put it in a plastic bag, the plastic would rip when I took it down, but the original packing would be intact.

Leaving the laptop box, I rummaged through the bottom

drawer for tape and stopped when I found an old photo of Marilyn and me. It was taken the same year we had married, at an event commemorating the one-year anniversary of Senator White's election.

The Ritz Grand Ballroom was packed. I said to Marilyn, "I should've raised the minimum donation to get in tonight."

She smiled. "You did fine, darling. There's always a way to raise more when you need it."

A photographer knelt before us as a reporter from the *Wall Street Journal* approached. I wrapped my arm around Marilyn and smiled for the picture. The reporter said, "Good evening, Mrs. Boggs. Mind if I borrow your husband for a quick interview?"

"Not at all. I'll see you later, Gideon." She pecked my cheek and made a beeline to Pam Biondi, Florida's Attorney General.

"This is quite an affair you've put together, Mr. Brighthouse."

"People enjoy supporting the senator."

"What can you tell us about the senator's plans?"

"Senator White is working on a bipartisan plan with Senator Blalock to resolve the immigration stalemate."

"That's a difficult subject to tackle, but I'm interested in what his plans are for higher office."

The rumors that had begun to circulate made me tingle, but I had to be careful. "The senator is focused on the second year of his six-year term."

"That's noble, but there's a rising chorus who say the senator should run for president."

"While that's a flattering proposal, the senator is committed to serving the good people of Florida and intends to serve his full term."

"What if the movement grows? Would the senator consider making a run for the White House?"

Marilyn was dancing with the aging patriarch of the Collier family and smiled as she sashayed by.

"This all makes for interesting speculation, but I'd like to get back to my wife before old boy Collier steals her."

I headed to Marilyn and chatted with Collier before whispering in her ear, "The word's out. All the *Journal* wanted to talk about was White making a bid for the White House."

She squeezed me. "Oh, Gideon, can you imagine? That would be wonderful."

"I know, it'd be amazing, and we'd help make sure it happened."

I tossed the picture back in the drawer, wondering how we got to the point where she was having affairs and I wanted her dead.

WE REACHED a tipping point three years ago in March. Senator White was holding a rally at the Naples Grand Resort that I'd arranged, and Marilyn hadn't shown up for it. I called her several times, but she never picked up. Our campaign had been playing nonstop defense since a pay-for-play scandal had broken. White had sponsored some agriculture legislation that would give disproportionate benefits to his largest donor. The blowback was ferocious. White couldn't get his talking points across, forcing us to double our efforts to push his agenda.

The ballroom had zero energy that night. It was the fifth lackluster event in a long week. I was tired and in no mood to stick around for a post-event evaluation. As soon as White went up to his room, I said my goodbyes, telling everyone Marilyn wasn't feeling good and drove home.

I can still see her on the bedroom chaise reading. Entering the room, I asked, "Where were you? I needed you to be there. You're making me look bad."

She shook her head. "You don't get it, do you?"

"Get what, Marilyn?"

She silently picked her book up and began reading.

"Stop playing games, will you?"

Never taking her eyes from the book, she said, "You're wasting your time with White. He's finished."

I hated her dismissiveness. "What are you talking about? We're just getting the campaign started."

"You're talking like a fool, Gideon. People are running from him."

"That's not true."

Placing the book in her lap, she said, "Really? How busy was your event?"

She had a point. The ballroom was just about a third filled. "It was okay, they'll come around."

She laughed, "Wait till you see tomorrow's editorial."

What did she know? How could she not inform me? "What are you talking about?"

"Let's just say it's safe to say he doesn't have many friends left."

"Well, if they leave him at the first sign of trouble, they weren't friends to begin with. Where's their loyalty?"

"There is where you're wrong again. You've got to run at the first hint of rot."

"That's not how I operate."

"That's the difference between you and me, Gideon. The Boggs never associate themselves with failure."

It was a verbal stomach punch, a dreadful revelation that

exemplified the difference in our DNA. I hoped it wasn't permanent, but when I woke up on the couch the next morning, the reality that things had changed haunted me.

I tried to bridge the gap, but the relationship continued to erode, albeit at a slower pace. Then my heart attack hit and what remained of the relationship quickly disintegrated into full-blown dysfunction.

12

RAUL SANCHEZ

TAKING THE STAIRS TO ALEJANDRO'S APARTMENT, MY LEGS felt heavy. Why was I so tired? The heat here was no worse than Mexico. My job on Keewaydin was physical but nothing crazy. Everybody says it's the stress from mama's cancer. Maybe. But what about the stress of toeing the line with so many chances for easy money?

Alejandro's was on the third floor. He was another fool, cleaning offices at night and cutting lawns in the day. A cat ran by. I tried to kick it, then knocked on the door.

"Hey Raul."

"What the doctor say?"

Alejandro frowned. "She's weaker. Doctor says your mama needs more dialysis."

"When she getting it?"

He shook his head. "They said Medicare won't pay for more."

"What?"

"Said she gets what everyone else gets."

"But he said she needs more, no?"

"Yeah."

"So, what's next?"

Alejandro shrugged. "He said you could pay, but it's like six grand a month."

"RAUL, GRAB ME ANOTHER FLAT."

I pulled the last flat of begonias off the trailer and took them to Pedro, asking, "How many people they having?"

"I dunno, man."

I said, "I can't believe we're ripping these pansies out. Who's coming, the fucking president?"

"Charlie said somethin' about a charity thing."

"Charity? With all the shit they throw out around here?"

"I know what you mean, man. But they got money."

"It ain't right, especially when they throw out food."

Pedro planted another begonia and said, "I asked the jefe one day if we could have the leftovers, but he said no."

"Me too, he told me to mind my business." I mopped my brow. "Pena's got no balls, man."

"Last place I was at, they always gave food to us when they had parties."

"It's a fucking waste."

"It's the way it is, man."

"They're sticking it in our faces."

"I know. Hey, amigo, go get more flowers."

Pushing the trailer, I slow-walked it to the dock. If it weren't for Mama, I would've ditched everything. Grabbed me what I could. She needed me, she's sick. And now she needed big money for dialysis. Man, the way I knew to get serious money was by doing what put me behind bars.

If I got nailed again, I knew what would happen. Me, I could handle being in the joint, but it'd kill mama. Locked up in Mexico, she came every week, but each time she looked a shitload older. If I went back in, it'd kill her before the kidney cancer did. There had to be a way to get the cash to help her.

I loaded the trailer, thinking it wasn't easy staying straight. A big-assed yacht, music blaring, sped by. Man, some people had it easy, just like the Boggs woman. Born on third base and the bitch thinks she hit a triple. She's got more money than God. You know, she could fix this shit fast. I'm gonna lean on her. How can she say no?

THE DECK HAD MORE chairs than a hotel. I looked for places to touch up, keeping my eye on the sliders. She usually left the house after lunch. Moving a club chair, I saw her in the window by the sink. Grabbing the paint can, I went to the window.

Boggs saw me. She smiled, and I put up a finger, beckoning her. Her smile disappeared and she stepped back. I held up my paint brush and she relaxed, opening the slider. A blast of cold air hit me.

"How can I help you?"

"I'm sorry, ma'am. But I—I need to ask you something."

She leaned away from the door but said nothing.

"Uhm, you see it's about my mama."

"You're Raul, correct?"

I nodded. "I work with Senor Pena."

She smiled. "Tell me. What's happening with your mother?"

"You see, she's got cancer, in the kidney."

Boggs frowned. "I'm so sorry."

"I know, and it's bad, real bad."

"It must be difficult for you."

"It is."

"How can I help? Would you like Mr. Pena to give you time to be with your mother?"

"She needs dialysis. More dialysis."

"Raul, I'm sure if that is what the doctor prescribes, it's nothing to be fearful of."

"But she can't have it."

She almost reached for my hand. "I know it's frightening to see your mother go through this, but dialysis, as serious as it is, is what she needs and you shouldn't be afraid of it."

"We want it, but we don't have the money."

A diamond earring appeared as Boggs tilted her head. "Doesn't she have insurance?"

"She got Medicare, but they only give her once a week, and doctor says mama needs more."

"I understand. There's an appeal process when people are denied treatment."

"She'll be dead by then."

She pursed her lips. "I see. Maybe there's something we can do for your mother. Let me talk to the office and see what can be arranged."

THE BOAT DROPPED me and the rest of the maintenance crew back on the mainland. I got in my car, slamming the door. A couple of days had passed, and that bitch never answered me. Who the hell do these people think they are?

I threw gravel leaving the parking lot and headed east. Needing a brew, I stopped in a Seven Eleven. I bought a six-pack, guzzling half a can before getting in the car. Driving around, I tried to think things out. But except for one time, I'd kept things square, and where'd it get me?

By the time I got to our shithole, there were five crushed cans on the floor. Ripping the ring off the last beer, I couldn't shake that Boggs was playing with me.

She even had the gall to give me the shit she felt bad mama was sick. I almost believed her, but it was just a game. She shouldn't fool with me. The bitch didn't know who she was fucking with. I drained the last can, watching Alejandro drag trash cans to the curb. The sucker was taking the whole building out. I got out of the car.

"Yo, Alejandro. You wanna take mine out?"

"Hey, Raul. We need to talk."

"What of?"

"Your mama."

"What about her?"

"It's not good. The doctor's worried."

"About what?"

"Something about her blood. Said she really needs more of the dialysis."

"Those fucks should just give it to her then."

He shrugged. "I know."

"This shit's all fucked up, man."

"We gotta do somethin'"

"I'm gonna handle it."

"Whaddya mean?"

"Later, Alejandro."

WALKING TO OUR PLACE, I told myself to be smart about things. There was easy money to be made, big money. It was all sitting right there, asking to be taken, but I couldn't get greedy. I'd go at it slowly, take a couple of pieces and see how it goes.

I hesitated before pulling the screen door open, trying to hear if mama was up. This was one night I hoped she was sleeping. The TV was on, but mama was sleeping in her recliner. I lowered the volume and she stirred.

"Raul?"

"Go back to sleep, Mama."

She tried to get up. "I make you . . . something."

I put my hand on her bony shoulder, "Stay, Mama; rest."

She fell back into the chair. "I'm so tired."

"It's okay, Mama. It's gonna be okay."

"The doctors say . . . I need more . . ."

"I know, Mama. I'm gonna get it for you. Don't worry."

Pecking her cheek, I fixed her blanket and said good night.

I went to my tiny room. I grabbed a backpack and stuffed a black T-shirt and black chinos in it. Standing on the bed, I reached to the back of the closet shelf and pulled down a duffel bag. Making sure the blinds were closed, I dumped it out on my bed.

The small pile glinted in the lamplight. I grabbed my favorite, a jet-black Colt .45 and pointed it at the cracked mirror. It was too much firepower for such a soft job, but you had to be ready. Being with the Latin Kings, I knew you can never have too much muscle.

I slipped the gun and a blade in the backpack and put the other weapons back in the closet.

13

GIDEON BRIGHTHOUSE

I GENERALLY STEERED CLEAR OF THE MAIN HOUSE ON Wednesdays. It was the day Marilyn would bring her play-mate, currently smooth-talking John Barnet, to the island. From the outset, I didn't like Barnet, and I initially tried to keep Marilyn from doing business with him. He was a real showman, and I guess that's why she ended up being drawn to him. Who puts a liquor store in Waterside Shops? No way he can make any money, in my opinion.

Wine was a tough business, I was always told. People who knew, said beer was where the money came in to pay the bills, and trust me, no one is going to Waterside to pick up a six-pack, even if it's craft beer. Barnet spent a fortune outfit-ting the space his store occupied. Where'd he get that money from? When Marilyn started doing business with him, I had the family office make discreet inquiries into his past. There wasn't much. He was from Los Angeles, had a couple of liquor stores where the clerks were behind plexiglass, and the biggest sellers were fifths of Jim Beam.

Barnet always wore a pin, even when not wearing a jacket, to signify he was a sommelier. It shouted insecurity and made me suspicious. The office verified he'd attended L.A.'s National Wine School, achieving the lowest certification possible. There were four levels of certification, and you needed a level three certification to get a pin. I mentioned it to Marilyn, but she accused me of being jealous. She was partially right; I was envious of his wine knowledge. I wanted to see him challenged on it, but since almost everyone knew less than him, it never happened.

Knowing wine and making money from it, at least in the Los Angeles neighborhoods where he did business, were two different things. It was a puzzle I'd wasted energy on because I saw how he captivated my wife, and I believed he sucked it out of from another rich woman.

I was feeling good about my plan. A side benefit would be I'd never see Barnet again. If those two knew what was coming, they wouldn't be cavorting around. They knew I was on the island, but they pretended they were alone. I was tired of being made a fool. They'd change it up if they knew their affair was going to come to a screeching halt this weekend.

On Saturdays there was only one housekeeper, and she always did the pool house around the time Marilyn would finish her yoga class. I'd put the mushroom into her juicer when she went to get the coconut milk, and that would be it.

A rush surged through my body and I smiled. I hadn't felt this good since before the heart attack. Believing I should have done her in a year ago, I got up and headed to the main house. For some reason I wanted to see them together; maybe it was my conscience demanding reinforcement.

The tennis courts were visible in the distance. They had blue Har-Tru surfaces, and an image of Marilyn and me playing there in our tennis whites morphed into nurses tending to her when she slipped into a coma. Nothing I had read fixed the amount of time she'd be in a coma before dying. The average seemed to be three days. I hoped it would be quicker, but certainly not suddenly.

Going up the stairs two steps at a time, I heard voices that seemed to be arguing and were coming from the family room. I slowed down. No need to announce my presence; I wanted to surprise them. Slipping through the front door into the bleached, wood-paneled foyer, I stopped in front of a Ralph Lauren mirror which reflected the couple. Wine glasses in hand, Marilyn was on the beige Chesterfield couch, and opposite her Barnet sat on the blue bench in front of the grand piano.

Barnet was outfitted in light blue pants and a white linen shirt that made his deep tan look too dark. I squinted. Was he wearing orange socks? Waiting till he was in the midst of a sip, I stepped into the room,

"Wow. Am I witnessing a lover's quarrel?"

Barnet nearly choked and stood up, towering over Marilyn, who said, "Gideon. You remember John."

"How could I forget? He's the guy who's been screwing you, for what, over a year now?"

Barnet stiffened. "I—I better be going."

"Ah, come on, John, stay. I don't want to be the one to break up the weekly screw fest."

Marilyn said, "That's enough, Gideon!"

Barnet said, "Look, I'm gonna get going."

Marilyn said, "Don't you dare."

I said, "Say, John, that pin of yours, I believe you need more than just the entry-level class to earn one."

Barnet's eyes moved to his chest and he said, "The sommelier pin? Technically there are several levels of certification. When things got too busy, I stopped taking courses and ended up somewhere in the middle."

"Really? As far as I know, you only passed the first level in L.A., which doesn't entitle you to a pin."

"I took additional classes with their Parisian affiliate."

"Real smooth, aren't you? You've got an answer for everything."

Marilyn sprung off the sofa. "Damn you, Gideon."

Barnet said, "I'm sorry to have upset you, Gideon."

"Me, upset? Why would you being here, in my living room, with my wife, upset me? It's your Wednesday routine, isn't it?"

Marilyn got up, saying, "Calm yourself down, Gideon. You're making a fool of yourself."

I laughed, "Really, and all the time I thought it was the two of you making me out to be a damn idiot. How silly of me."

Barnet turned to Marilyn. "It's better if I leave."

I headed for the door. "No need to. The house is all yours."

They'd gotten way too comfortable and needed a conscience check. Having both of them squirm a little before Marilyn left the scene forever felt damn good.

14

GIDEON BRIGHTHOUSE

IMAGES OF MARILYN AND JOHN BARNET HAVING SEX THAT afternoon haunted me. The doctors told me to take a walk when I was agitated to help calm me down. I slid a door open, stepping into a breeze that was sprinkled with rain, and retreated.

Those bastards probably did it in my old bedroom, the sexual pleasure heightened by the excitement from the encounter with me. Marilyn was so smug this afternoon, and that Barnet, he was a shifty bloodsucker if there ever was one. He played it right, though, much as I hate to admit. He offered two, or was it three times to leave? Barnet didn't antagonize me at the time and even looked like he was some-what scared. It was probably all an act. What was that Parisian nonsense? I'd have to check that out; he was prob-ably lying.

Why did I give a damn what they did? In less than three days I'd have a fresh canvas to paint my life on. Still, no matter how hard I tried, I couldn't shake them from my mind, especially Marilyn. As the rage rose, I tried the breathing exercises and the new stretching regime, but nothing worked.

Two of my pill bottles and a glass of water were on the coffee table. It was just past seven thirty. The Valium and Ativan combo had knocked me out. I'd been sleeping a couple of hours. I sat up, drank the rest of the water, and waited for the fog to lift.

When my mind cleared, I grabbed *Contemporary Art Monthly* off the coffee table and flipped through it to an article on Jasper Johns. About halfway through, the piece mentioned a string of his lesser-known works, and I was certain that the author had mistitled a small painting. Setting the magazine down, I lowered the recliner and headed to Serenity House. The library in the main house held every art book I'd ever owned, and among the wall-to-wall shelves a retrospective of Johns waited to clarify the title.

Approaching, I noticed that no lights, other than the automatics, were on. All six pairs of double windows above the front porch were ebony mirrors. Unless she left when I had slept, Marilyn was home. Perhaps she'd fallen asleep after her session with Barnet. I considered yelling her name out to wake her as I turned into the library.

The room was another sanctuary for me. Every inch of the library was lined with ceiling-to-floor, blond wood shelves. Ladders on each wall, that glided on brushed nickel rails, broke up the reams of books. The room's massive size was mitigated by three comfortable seating areas. I grabbed the retrospective I was looking for and was about to plop into my favorite wing chair, when I realized the dim sound I was hearing was running water.

I headed into the kitchen. Sure enough, the water was running in the island sink. Coming around the island, my hands flew up, and as the book tumbled to the floor, I shouted, "Oh my God!"

Stepping over a stream of blood, I knelt and felt Marilyn's neck for a pulse. She was stiff and cold. Jumping up, I looked around. A bloody kitchen knife was on the floor a few feet away. I stepped over her body, shut the water off, and stared at Marilyn as my heart began to pound. Turning away from her, I began to run, kicking the book as I left the kitchen. When I got to the pool house, I grabbed my pills and choked, trying to down two without water. A dizzy feeling came over me and I tried to fight it with my breathing exercises but was overcome by blackness.

WHEN I WOKE, I was on the floor. My head was pounding and my wrist was sprained. I scrambled to my feet. Was it all a dream? It had to be. The conscience can be vicious, I knew. It's the only thing that keeps the world from descending into total chaos. This had to be a warning. Didn't it? My mind was telling me not to go through with killing Marilyn.

I left the pool house and tiptoed my way to Serenity. The front door was wide open. I pulled out my cell phone and headed in.

15

LUCA

Lights illuminating the way ahead, a police boat pushed off Naples City Dock. It navigated slowly until entering Naples Bay, where it sped up considerably.

Passing inlets of black water that led to Port Royal, lights outlining the enclave known as Keewaydin Island became visible. I took a step toward the bow and said, "Talk about privileged? This is off the hook."

Vargas said, "How many people live on it, Luca?"

"Pretty sure it's just Marilyn Boggs and her husband."

"Really? Looks like there's five, six buildings, at least. Just for the two of them?"

I nodded. "According to Susan. She and her husband own 'Sweet Liberty'. Did you ever take a ride on their catamaran?"

"No."

"You should. It's beautiful. Anyway, she said when the Boggs bought it they built three houses for themselves. And there's a guesthouse, a pool house, and, get this, a building for all their art."

"That's over the top. It looks so peaceful. I've never been on the island."

"Well, there's another thing for you to do. You know, for a Floridian, you don't seem to know as much as I do about the area."

"You know how it goes. People who live in New York never go to the Statue of Liberty, right?"

I nodded. "Anyway, seventy-five percent of the island is owned by the State of Florida. I took a boat ride over there about a year ago. It's real peaceful, gazillions of wildlife. The day I went, I saw at least half a dozen bald eagles. Keeway-din's got a real shelly beach, so bring your sneakers if you go."

A couple of yachts filled with onlookers were drifting fifty yards off the island's shoreline. Our boat slowed down as it approached the dock, maneuvering into a space between four powerboats that were tied up. Two of them were police boats and had their strobe lights on.

Vargas said, "The husband found the body?"

"Yeah, he called it in. Name's Gideon Brighthouse."

"Brighthouse? Thought the family name was Boggs."

"It is. Apparently, the wife never took his name. The chief said Brighthouse was a political operative awhile back, used to work for one of Florida's senators."

"Then he jumped on the gravy train?"

"Maybe. We'll find out if it was the money or that elusive thing we call love."

"Speaking of romance, how are things with Kayla? I thought you said she was coming into town."

"Yeah, she was supposed to be heading in for a couple of days, but something came up and she had to cancel." I couldn't tell Vargas I thought Kayla was brushing me off, it'd be embarrassing considering how I'd made it seem things were going great."

"Oh."

The last thing I needed to think about now was Kayla. I pushed the blue feeling aside and focused on the new case.

"Let's see what we've got here."

I helped Vargas off the boat onto a long, gray dock made of Trex. Thirty feet away a gate of scrolled iron, with pickets overhanging the water, prevented anyone from getting from the dock onto the island. It was a measure of security, but that didn't mean someone couldn't swim in off a boat.

After examining the area around the dock, I surveyed the house. A dozen royal palms, beautifully lit, lined a wide, stone path to the Key West-styled home. Man, I couldn't even come up with a number for what this place was worth. I wished it were daylight. We'd have to come back in the morning, and I'd get a bead on what this place looked like.

Two men were heading our way down the lighted walkway. I knew from the suit and strut that one of them was a lawyer. He barely nodded to us and went past us, straight toward the police boats.

I introduced ourselves to Frank Flynn. In white boat sneakers, shorts, and a tee shirt, Flynn was a family friend who was carrying forty pounds of extra weight. After telling me I looked like George Clooney, he revealed that he lived across the strait in Port Royal and had been summoned by the family lawyer. Flynn said Gideon, the husband, was distraught and in the pool house. As we made our way to the main house, he told us that he'd been the first to arrive and that he met Gideon at the dock but did not see the body.

It was the first murder scene I'd approached without having a microphone stuck in my face. However, that wasn't the extent of how different this one was. Usually there were plenty of patrol cars, a perimeter line set up around the actual scene, and another further out to fence off an area, preventing the media and public from interfering. Here, we were surrounded by a gulf barely lapping at the shore, under a black sky speckled with diamonds. It was quiet, and if not for the police boat lights, a perfect spot to honeymoon.

Peter Gerey caught up with us after convincing the police boats to tone down their lights. Serious as cancer, Gerey was the lawyer who quarterbacked the family's interests in the State of Florida. A partner in a small firm, he helped guide the top one-tenth of a percent on matters of money, privacy, and that good old intangible, reputation.

Thin-lipped, Gerey spoke in the hushed tone of an undertaker.

"Detective, the family would appreciate discretion in regards to the press. We'd like to avoid having to combat baseless rumors. I trust you realize the Boggs are a prominent family, one that employs hundreds of people. Despite their profile in the community, the Boggs family places a high value on their privacy."

I held up a hand. "Counselor, I'm here to conduct an investigation. Talking to the press isn't a part of my job description. I'm sure you know a bunch of people at the sheriff's office, and I'd suggest that's where you make your pitch. Now, this is as far as you can go."

"But—"

"No "buts." This is a crime scene."

We climbed the stairs to the porch, and over the door was a hand-carved sign with silver lettering: Serenity House. I thought about the coming contradiction as we signed in with the officer guarding the scene.

16

LUCA

I STOOD IN THE FOYER. IT WAS A MAGNIFICENT HOME, THE nicest I'd ever been in. There were a lot of interesting pictures hanging with little lights over them. But it wasn't like the place was a museum. It was tough to explain; you just knew it was expensive, but it wasn't gaudy. It was, it hit me, serene.

Well, all that serenity was broken, as usual, by human behavior gone off the rails. The sound of a camera snapping and whirring away prompted me to pull on booties and gloves and get to work.

The officer standing in the kitchen entranceway said the coroner was expected within the hour. He moved aside and we stepped into the kitchen. It looked like one of those kitchens you see in design magazines.

White quartz topped the gray cabinets along the walls, and the island had the reverse, white cabinets and a gray slab on top. The body wasn't visible, and if not for the uniforms, it could have been the cleanup after an elegant dinner party. A slight coffee smell hung in the air, and my gaze wandered to cabinetry that housed built-in espresso and Keurig machines.

The photographer, a good kid named Giancarlo, stood up. He was finished. I asked him to find out how to turn on all the outside lights and see if there were any footprints he could document in case a rainstorm came through.

Vargas and I sidestepped over an art book, and there was the body.

Marilyn Boggs, a small woman with a pixie haircut, looked almost ten years younger than the fifty I was told she was. She was on her back, head lolled to the left, and was wearing jewelry that weighed more than she did. One of her stilettos was half off, and her skirt was hiked, revealing a thin thigh. She wasn't my type.

Stepping over a stream of blood, I crouched down. Gravity had begun to pool her blood. She'd been dead more than a couple of hours. Her perfect makeup was marred by smudged lipstick and a slight mark on her right cheek. The woman's upper body was resting on a puddle of crimson red that was getting gummy. A single puncture wound in her chest, that I figured went completely through her thin body, was the source of the puddle.

I stood. "She's five foot one, max. We'll get a good idea from the wound how tall the killer was."

A long, serrated knife with an ebony handle lay three feet to the right of the body. Tinged red, it looked to be the murder weapon. How did this rich lady end up dead? The knife, unusual in the wealthy circles of crime, was puzzling. Stabbings were rare; this could be a break-in gone bad.

I glared at two officers who were talking like they were at a tailgate party.

"Come on, guys!"

Vargas said, "Why don't you two wait in the hallway?"

The officers backed out of the kitchen, and Vargas said,

"Crazy, all this money, and she's stabbed like a hooker in an alleyway."

"Money? This isn't money, Vargas. This is what's called wealth."

She shook her head. "Money, wealth, whatever. It can't buy you happiness or, apparently, security."

I circled around to the other side of the kitchen, visualizing how a struggle may have played out. She was on the floor near one of those double-basin farm sinks. The woman could have been at the sink and was surprised by someone. Maybe he came through one of the massive sliders that formed the left-hand wall, which overlooked an outdoor dining area and fountain.

A lone wine glass, delicately thin and empty, sat on the island. I took a closer look at the glass. The rim appeared clean and the glass didn't show any signs of residue. A few feet to the left, a bottle of red wine, three-quarters empty, was sitting on top of a white marble disk.

To the left of the glass and disassembled, was an expensive-looking juicer. I checked it for traces of water for a clue to when it had been cleaned.

There was an empty slot in the bleached-wood knife block sitting on the counter two feet from the sink, which was also empty. Looking at the handles, it was clear that was where the murder weapon came from. How did the murderer get their hands on it if she was in the kitchen?

"What are you thinking, Luca?"

"Was the victim in the kitchen, or was she out of the room and a thief came in? Then she surprised him, and he went for the knife?"

"I don't know; this is not the easiest place to rob."

"Agreed, but it could've been someone on staff or some worker, who knows? Either way, we've got a ton of interviewing to conduct. First thing: find out who was on the island, who came and went, and if anyone saw or heard a boat close by."

"Didn't you say the island is mostly owned by the state?"

"Yeah, that's right."

"Is it possible someone got on the island from that side?"

"Absolutely."

Vargas sighed. "I thought the remoteness of this place would make the investigation easy."

"Easy? The last easy case I was on was . . . oh yeah, there never was one, unless you want to count a burglary one time where this guy broke in, got drunk, and fell asleep. The husband found him and called us."

"You never told me about that."

"No end to the madness in this business."

"You want to interview the husband now? He's in the pool house."

"Let's take a look at the master bedroom first. We'll check the rest of the place after we talk to him."

A stairway of glass and iron, providing a nice dose of modernity, emptied into a loft-like family room that served a bank of bedrooms to the right. A sitting area where the hallway split, led to double doors, signaling the master bedroom suite.

Expecting a concert hall-sized bedroom, I was surprised by the coziness of the room, which was anchored by a modern, king-sized bed. A large picture of a colorful triangle that reminded me of the album cover for *Dark Side of the Moon* hung opposite the bed.

It looked like one side of the bed had been slept in, and the bedding simply straightened.

I said, "Looks like someone slept alone last night."

"Maybe they were fighting and things escalated today."

"We'll find out soon enough."

I checked both of the gray nightstands before a pair of French doors drew me to a rear-facing deck. Sticking my head outside, I wondered how nice it would be to wake up to such a panoramic view. The deck furniture gave no indication of activity, so I closed the door.

"Nothing out there. Let's check the rest."

We stepped into her closet, which had more square footage than the bedroom. There were three modern takes on chandeliers hanging from the ceiling and a mirrored vanity that ran for at least fifteen feet. The closet had four sections, each divided by a small, modern picture: makeup, hanging garments, shoe storage, and banks of drawers.

Vargas said, "This is what most women call heaven."

I passed rows and rows of custom shoe shelving. "There's gotta be two hundred pairs or more here. This is crazy."

"Not if you can afford it."

In the long-hang section there were more gowns than most bridal stores, but not much color variety. It was clear Mrs. Boggs was a fan of white, black, and gray, especially in formal wear. The medium, mid-medium, and short-hang sections offered a more colorful palette but no clues.

It took us a half hour to search all the drawers, but we ended up with nothing and moved to the husband's closet, which was materially smaller but more than ample.

"The guy gets screwed again."

"What?"

"It's like, not even half the space."

Vargas pointed to a couple of large gaps in the hanging area. "He's not even using what he has."

"My bet is he's living somewhere else. Maybe in one of the other houses."

"How many do they have?"

"I don't know, but you can bet with this kind of wealth they have more than one house."

Vargas pulled open drawers. "You're right, only a handful of things."

The palatial bathroom featured a walk-in shower where you could play handball, and a freestanding tub that was egg-shaped. Straddling the edge of the white tub was a wooden tray designed to hold two Champagne flutes.

"I got to get me one of those."

Her vanity had a tray with an assortment of brushes and an electric toothbrush sitting in its charger. Pulling the clear plastic cap off the toothbrush head, I brushed it over the bristles. I noted the droplets of water the action produced and moved on.

The male vanity top was empty. I pulled opened the top drawer and squeezed the toothpaste. It had hardened.

"Come on, let's have our chat with Mr. Boggs."

We left the main house as the forensics team arrived.

17

LUCA

As we gave instructions to the officers guarding the scene, Peter Gerey was pacing in the distance, talking on his phone. He noticed us and hurried over as we asked the officers to inform us when the coroner arrived.

"Did you find anything, Detective?"

"Now Counselor, you know we can't share that information. This is an active investigation."

"It wasn't an attempt for inside information, Detective. I understand the rules of the game. My concern and hence inquiry is for the family, their privacy and reputation."

Sure. It couldn't be the five hundred an hour guys like you charge, Luca thought.

"Noted. We'd like to speak with Gideon Brighthouse."

"Of course. Mr. Brighthouse is in the pool house." Gerey pointed to a two-story structure that stood to the left of a rectangular pool, its lights changing from blue to purple.

I loved the way the breeze felt on my face as we made our way. The pool house sat in between the main house and the guesthouse, each generously separated with landscaping and setbacks. Since the entire private side of the island was technically a crime scene, it left us with a lot of property to comb through. I didn't think so, but who knew? Maybe even the water surrounding this place would need to be searched.

As the stone path meandered to the pool, lights illuminated a sliver of the beach, highlighting uniform lines that said the beach was raked. I wasn't much of a nighttime swimmer, but the pool, now lit a reddish color, began whispering to me as we reached its decking.

The entire first floor of the building was a series of ten-foot sliding doors, giving the impression that the second floor was floating above. As we entered an open slider, a cascade of rustling palm trees filled the air. Frank Flynn, seated across from Gideon Brighthouse, struggled to get off a white leather sofa.

Brighthouse waited until Flynn took at least five steps toward us before standing. Was that strategic or plain old superiority? Gerey stepped ahead, whispered to his client, and introduced him,

"Detectives, this is Gideon Brighthouse."

Gideon had delicate features and hazy blue eyes. His wavy hair, on the long side, seemed prematurely gray, unless he'd had work done like his wife. He was tall, over six foot for sure, and his long legs stuck way out of his pink shorts. He didn't offer his hand. The call between superiority and germaphobia was easy, but he just didn't look like one of those high-minded, 'shit-don't-stink' guys.

Vargas said, "We're sorry about your loss, Mr. Brighthouse."

As he nodded, Gerey said, "If you're up to it, Gideon, they'd like to speak with you, but only if you feel up to it."

Gideon whispered, "I guess so."

Flynn herded us around a glass-topped table before Gerey asked him to leave. To the right, a linear fireplace threw off just the right amount of heat to offset the breeze blowing through the house.

Vargas said, "Again, please accept our condolences, but we need to ask you some questions."

Gideon glanced at Gerey, who nodded.

"Can you tell us what happened?"

Gideon pulled his head back. "Happened? Nothing happened. I just found her, lying there, she was . . . dead. I checked to see if she had a pulse or anything, but . . . there wasn't any."

"What time was this?"

"Uh, about seven thirty."

"You sure?"

Gideon nodded.

"Where were you before you found the body?"

"The library. I'd come in to get one of my art books and . . . I heard the sound of running water. I thought someone had left the water on, and we need to save all the water we can on the island, so I went into the kitchen and . . . oh my God, there she was."

"Was the water on?"

"The water?"

"You said you heard water running."

"I did, I think so. Yes, it was running."

"Which sink?"

"Uh, the island one."

"Did you shut off the water?"

Gideon looked at Gerey. "What difference does all this make?"

I said, "Mr. Brighthouse, it may seem irrelevant, but we need to piece together events, and it's a detail that may be helpful. Did you shut the water off?"

Gideon hesitated. "I honestly don't remember. I really don't."

I wondered if he was calculating the difference as Gerey said, "That's perfectly normal, Gideon. You've been traumatized by a brutal, unthinkable act of violence."

Vargas said, "Okay. You see your wife lying on the floor bleeding and check her vitals."

Gideon nodded.

Vargas said, "What did you do next?"

His shoulders slumped a bit. "I, uh, ran out of the house."

"You didn't call for help?"

"She was dead."

"How could you be sure?"

Gideon squirmed in his chair. "I didn't know what to do. I . . . my heart started to pound. I've had one heart attack already, and I—I just had to get out of there."

Gerey said, "Mr. Brighthouse has been diagnosed with an anxiety disorder and is under a doctor's care."

"I understand."

Maybe it was because my pee-pee alarm vibrated that I said, "Where did you run off to?"

Gerey glared at me. "There's no need to phrase it that way, Detective."

"Trust me, there was nothing intended by the way I said it. Where did you go when you left the kitchen?"

"I went straight to my house."

"Your house?"

He seemed to gulp for air. "Here, I meant the pool house."

Between the bed and the house reference, I didn't need him to spell anything out. This was looking like another domestic murder case. I didn't want to focus on him just yet, so I asked, "Did you see anything unusual at any time today?"

He started swaying in his chair. "Not that I recall."

Through the open doors I saw an officer approaching. The coroner must have arrived. I asked, "How about any sounds? Maybe a boat? Any screams?"

He shrugged. "There's no shortage of boats around here, but certainly no more than usual today. I can't recall anything that stood out."

"Give it some more thought and let us know."

He nodded. "I will."

I said, "We'll talk again. The coroner has arrived, and I always like to be on the scene when he does."

Before walking over to the main house, I hit the bathroom. Sitting and waiting to pee didn't bother me; this was one nice bathroom with a lot to take in.

18

LUCA

"WHAT THE HELL ARE THEY DOING?"

I ran toward the officers talking on the beach. "Hey, hey. Get off the sand!"

The officers froze like deer in the headlights.

"This is a private island with very little traffic. I don't want you guys mucking up the sand with your footprints if the killer came in off the beach."

I went back to Vargas as the officers tiptoed their way onto the grass.

"Unreal. You know, they should make a special force to respond to the scene of a homicide. You'd think they'd learn by now or at least use some damn common sense. But no, no, they just make our jobs tougher."

"Okay Frank, take it easy."

"The new sheriff we got, if he knows everything there is to know, how come he hasn't ordered a response team?"

"You're overreacting."

"It probably doesn't matter anyway. It's looking like Mr. 'My-Shit-Don't-Stink' did it."

"Don't you think it's a bit early?"

"I know that. Did you hear what he said about his house? They're not sleeping together. I know there are couples that have separate beds or even bedrooms, but Mr. Hoity-Toity lives in another house altogether."

"I don't know why you think this guy is such a snob. He seemed pretty normal to me."

"Ah, come on Vargas, are you kidding me?"

"What did he do that gave you such an impression?"

"Geez, how about we start with his name, Gideon. I mean, how many plumbers are named Gideon? And he had like an English accent, one of those upper-crust ones."

"English accent? You know, Frank, sometimes I really think you're crazy."

She was right; it wasn't an accent. It was just the way he spoke, like highly enunciated or something,

"Crazy? Nah, I like to think of myself as interesting."

As we followed the travertine path to the main house, I said, "Check with the phone company, both the landline and her cell. Find out when the last calls were made and to who. Might help us with a time of death."

"I'm on it. Be a good idea to check on any credit card use as well, you never know."

"Sure, and I need you to track down the maids who work here and get them over here in the morning. The house needs a thorough going-over to see if anything is missing. We'll need to have Mr. Ivy League take a look as well."

"So, you haven't made up your mind after all?"

"Covering all the bases as usual. We gotta eliminate in order to focus."

GEORGE SHIELDS WAS HUNCHED over the body, pushing his thumb slowly through Marilyn's short hair.

The coroner for Collier County hated interruptions, and I had to bite my tongue to keep from firing questions at him. Doctor Shields unbuttoned the top of Marilyn's blouse. Moving to the left, I saw a wound crusted with blood.

Shields took each of her hands and examined them closely, then laid them by her side. As he rose, I said, "Find anything, Doc?"

"It doesn't look like there was much of struggle. She was stabbed once with a knife, probably the one right there, and bled to death. Her head has a sizable bruise, but I believe that's a result of a fall after the attack as she lost consciousness."

"Can you estimate the height of the killer?"

"Right now, I'd say he or she was tall, six feet plus."

"Right-handed or a lefty?"

"I can't say at this point. Need to get the victim on the table."

"How about a time of death?"

"I'd estimate death occurred about four hours ago. It's nine twenty now, so roughly anywhere from four to six."

Vargas and I exchanged glances.

Shields peeled off his gloves. "Moving the body on a boat is going to require extra precautions. I don't want the body being jostled around on the way in. The ride back has got to be slow and smooth."

"No problem, Doc. I'll come along with you. Mary Ann, why don't you take custody of the evidence we collected, and we'll meet up at the sheriff's office?"

Before heading to the dock, I gave instructions that no one, including the husband, was to be allowed near the main house.

WE HAD a new sheriff in town, and he was giving me grief. Frank Morgan was the virtual flip side to Joe Liberi, who took early retirement when he was diagnosed with lymphoma. Liberi knew I'd lost my partner and went out of his way to make the transition from Jersey as easy as possible. He appreciated the experience I brought down with me and appointed me as a quasi-mentor for those less seasoned.

I'd just returned to work after my battle with cancer, when Liberi was diagnosed. He was assured the treatment would be successful and allow him to keep working, but at sixty-two, he said it was time to move on and opted to retire. With the big C lurking over my shoulder, I was more than pleased that Liberi was now in remission. Perhaps that sorely-needed reassurance was the price I had to pay in the form of Frank Morgan.

Morgan had it in for anyone who wasn't from the South, and especially for anyone from the New York metro area. The first time I met him was at a barbecue at Liberi's house. Before making his retirement plans public, Liberi had organized a small gathering of who he considered key people to get to know his successor. I was honored to be one of six people Liberi invited but couldn't help thinking it was because of the cancer connection.

Morgan had been serving as the police chief for the City of Naples for the last twenty-two years. Its own municipality, the City of Naples had about twenty thousand citizens and policed its own streets. I knew a couple of officers who worked for Morgan. They said he ran a tight force and resented the growth that had transformed the town from a sleepy hamlet to a ritzy tourist destination.

Morgan was the poster boy for a country boy. He wore cowboy boots and those string ties that look like shoelaces. When he said he was born in Naples, I kiddingly asked if he was one of the ten people who were actually born here. He said, "You think that's funny, boy? You Northerners come down here trying to turn my town into some sort of a Times Square. Well, I promise you it won't happen on my watch." I didn't know what to say. I mean, how do you respond to something like that?

Catching Stewart for the Gabelli murder a week before Morgan took over, got me about halfway out of the hole I'd dug at the barbecue. I heard from a detective that Morgan had told him to reach out to me when he hit a dead end in a case. That felt good but did nothing to warm the air between us. The only thing on my side was time. Morgan was retiring himself and would only stay until the next election, when the people would choose a new sheriff.

It was nearly eleven o'clock when Vargas and I brushed past a handful of reporters and headed to the second-floor offices of the sheriff. The door to his office was wide open. Standing while talking on the phone, Morgan waved us in and moved behind his desk.

It felt good surveying the room. They only difference since Liberi occupied the office was the ten-gallon hat and holster hanging from the coat rack. We waited until he finished his call before sitting.

"I don't have to tell you how delicate this case is, do I?"

We said in unison, "No, sir."

Morgan nodded. "What am I dealing with here?"

I said, "The victim was—"

"Mind your manners, son. This is the South, where ladies still come first."

Vargas said, "Thank you, Sheriff, but Detective Luca and I agreed to have him lead this investigation."

"Go on then."

I said, "The victim was stabbed once and bled to death in the main home's kitchen. We believe we have recovered the murder weapon. There were no obvious signs of a break-in, but we plan to go over the property again. The husband said he discovered the body."

"Said? You have reason to believe he is lying?"

"Not exactly. Keewaydin Island presents a unique setting for a murder. It's very remote, thus limiting the universe of possible suspects."

He shook his head. "Me and my granddaddy used to fish right off of Key Island. Yep, we caught a whole lot of fish back in the days when the only boats off the homes in Port Royal were meant for fishing. You wouldn't know anything about that, would you, Luca?"

I noticed that Morgan used the island's old name. "Afraid not, sir."

"Anyone else besides Mr. Brighthouse on the island?"

"Not according to him. Said his wife gives the staff off on Wednesdays. At this point he's someone we're very interested in."

"Tread carefully. The Boggs family has been an important part of this community back to days when the state was formed. We can't be pointing fingers and dirtying reputations, you hear me?"

"Understood, sir. This is a serious crime, and we're going to conduct an exhaustive and thorough investigation."

"Good, but you've got to be discreet. You New York boys know what that word is, don't you?"

Vargas said, "We understand, sir."

"I don't want either of you talking to the press. They're

out there doing damn cartwheels with this story. I'll handle those rascals from here. Is that clear?"

Vargas and I nodded.

"I want to be kept fully apprised of the developments in this case. Now, get out of here and show me you're as good a detective as you think you are."

19

GIDEON BRIGHTHOUSE

AFTER WAKING, I STARTED MY CUSTOMARY FIFTEEN MINUTES of transcendental meditation while lying in bed. It was hard to quiet down, but the Maharishi was right, repeating a mantra is a bit of magic.

I said my last "om" and was feeling as balanced and peaceful as I could, considering the circumstances, and headed down to breakfast. I was hoping Shell had left a bowl of high-fiber cereal with my coffee and juice, as my body had completely shut down.

No cereal, but a heaping bowl of berries, and the juice was prune. I poured a cup of coffee, stirred in my skim milk and took a sip. Blood began pounding in my ears as soon as I unfolded the newspaper. I got up, ripped open a slider, and paced the pool deck, deeply inhaling the air and view of the gulf. The pounding receded and I waved back at Matthew, who was raking the beach.

If I'd thought about it, I shouldn't have been surprised by the headline in the *Naples Daily News* that blared, Socialite Marilyn Boggs Murdered at Home. Maybe it was the helicopter pictures of Keewaydin, with arrows naming the buildings on the island, stripping away a layer of privacy, that wobbled me. Needing an appointment to talk through all of this, I called my therapist and left a message before heading inside.

Pushing the paper to the far edge of the table, I ate breakfast. After pouring another cup of coffee, I dragged the paper over and read the lead story.

Socialite Marilyn Boggs Murdered at Home

Philanthropist Marilyn Boggs was found stabbed to death in her Keewaydin Island home last night. Marilyn Boggs is the daughter of Martin Boggs, the late founder of American Investments. Mrs. Boggs served on the board of numerous charitable organizations in Collier County and was currently in leadership positions with The Juvenile Diabetes Foundation and St. Vincent de Paul Society.

The Collier County Sheriff's department responded to a 911 call made about 9 p.m. last night and found the body of Mrs. Boggs in the kitchen of the main home.

A prominent socialite, Mrs. Boggs lived on the private side of the island with her husband, Gideon Brighthouse, who was an adviser to former Senator Robert White. It is believed that Mr. Brighthouse was on the island at the time of the fatal attack and did not suffer any injuries.

Keewaydin Island is a barrier island off the coast of Naples, and 85% of the island is public and managed by the Florida Coastal Office. Eight miles long, the island is free of cars and filled with abundant wildlife.

A spokesman for Sheriff Morgan called the crime shocking and disturbing and said the sheriff had made solving the crime a priority for the department.

Born in Naples, Marilyn Boggs was 50 years old and had

no children. She is survived by her brothers, Paul and Wesley Boggs, who reside in Boston. Funeral arrangements have not been announced."

20

LUCA

Intermittent pain in my abdomen convinced me not to wait, and I was sitting in my urologist's office instead of trying to solve the Boggs case. A year ago, I would have swallowed a handful of Tylenol, but after getting bladder cancer I couldn't take chances.

Maybe it was the irritating morning show host or my nerves, but in spite of the sign that prohibited cell phone use, I called Vargas. Digging my chin into my chest, I said, "What's going on, Vargas?"

"Aren't you at the doctors?"

"Yeah, I'm in the waiting room. You got anything?"

"Went through the house with the husband, but he didn't notice anything. He kept claiming nobody could keep track of all the stuff his wife bought."

"He didn't live there anyway. What about the maids?"

"I'm just about to go through with a housekeeper named Shell."

"Keep me posted. I'm going outta my mind waiting here."

"Don't worry, Frank. Take care of yourself first. The case will be here when you're done."

My name was called as I hung up, and I hustled to the window expecting to start my visit. The woman behind the window asked me, "Mr. Luca, did you see the sign?" She pointed to the cell phone prohibition.

I nodded sheepishly and she said, "But you didn't understand it?"

Head hanging, I went back to my chair. After a half hour passed, the door swung open and a nurse with a clipboard called my name. She showed me into an exam room, weighed me, and left, telling me the doctor would be right in.

Leafing through *Men's Health*, a text came in from Vargas:

'Jewelry missing. Talk when you're out.'

While punching in her number, the door swung open. Chart in hand, it was Doctor Peters.

"How are you, Mr. Luca?"

"I'm okay, Doc."

He looked over my chart. "You're experiencing abdominal pain?"

I nodded.

"Take off your shirt and lay down."

Unbuttoning from the top down, my anxiety crept up. Would this be a day that would be scorched into my memory bank, or forgotten like yesterday's morning coffee?

My back stuck to the paper on the table as Peters bent over me, pressing his fingers into my gut. He moved around in a clockwise, circular motion until he hit an area that made me grunt.

"Just hold still, Mr. Luca." He massaged the area and did some type of pinching in the area that made me uncomfortable.

"That's the spot. What's going on, Doc?"

"Sit up."

Sit up? Wasn't bad news better to deliver to someone lying down?

"It appears to be nothing more than some scar tissue that has formed adhesions on your abdominal muscles."

Phew! "That's all it is?"

"I believe so. We'll do an ultrasound to be sure."

Ugh, now I had to sweat another test out? "Can you do it here?"

"We have the equipment, but you'll have to schedule it."

My shoulders sagged. "I was hoping——"

"I can understand your apprehension after all you've been through, but I'm pretty certain you've got nothing to worry about."

I heard myself say, "Yeah, that's what the first doctor said."

Peters studied me for a second, checked his watch, and picked up the phone.

"Sue, I need to squeeze in an ultrasound. Is room four open?"

This was one of the few times being a wise guy got me anywhere, or did it? I could be speeding up hearing bad news.

———————

MY SHIRT WAS ONLY HALF BUTTONED as I dialed Vargas on the way out of the waiting room. I paced the parking lot as she explained, "The maid identified a necklace and three cocktail rings as missing."

"Is she sure?"

"Absolutely. Said one of the missing rings was Marilyn's favorite, a gift from her father."

"Can we estimate the value?"

"I've gotten several pictures of Mrs. Boggs wearing the pieces, and I'll get them down to Georgie for an estimate. It may not be anything, but we also found fifty thousand in cash in her nightstand."

"Fifty thousand? That sounds like a lot to me, but we're talking about the ultrarich here. It's probably their petty cash."

"Kinda what I thought."

I said, "Look, we've got to alert all known fences and pawn shops in Collier and Lee."

"In the works, all the way up to Orlando."

"Oh, ask Gideon what jewelers the family dealt with."

"Done. He told us they primarily dealt with Thalheimers but had bought things over the years from Bigham as well."

She'd thought of everything; it was good but depressing.

"Frank, you there?"

"Yeah. Good work. I'll see you at the office."

"How'd it go with the doctor?"

"All good, just some scar tissue."

Hopping in my car, I couldn't believe the case just did a chameleon on me. Was this a robbery gone wrong? How did a thief, and now murderer, get on and off Keewaydin without being noticed? We'd have to canvass everyone. Someone had to see a boat unless Gideon was in on it. Could he have let someone onto the island to kill his wife and let him take some expensive jewelry as payment? That would make it appear to be a robbery, and there would be no paper trail for paying the assassin.

As I turned onto Pine Ridge, a pinch in my gut brought me back to the doctor's visit. It was good news, but I realized the relief that nothing serious was happening with my new plumbing had lasted all of a minute. I tried to understand why, as scared as I had been going in, that I was ungrateful.

Sitting at the light to 41, I forced myself to believe it was because of the case, but as the light turned green, the truth hit me. I felt I was due a pass after everything I'd been through. The car in back of me beeped its horn, and I finally pressed the gas pedal down.

21

LUCA

THREE DAYS AFTER THE MURDER, I STEPPED OFF NAPLES PIER and onto a police boat for the ride to Keewaydin Island. Normally I'd never consent to an interview with someone I considered a suspect on their territory. However, using Gideon's anxiety issues and the publicity the case had already attracted, the Boggs attorney had asked us to conduct the interview on Keewaydin. I didn't fight it. The island was captivating, and I looked forward to visiting as we slowly pulled away from the dock.

The boat sped up as we passed through the area where the water wavered between brackish and salt. It was a perfect day to be on the water. The Gulf of Mexico was a sheet of glass, and there was only the hint of a breeze. The only negative was the glare. Though I had my Maui Jims on, it was still too bright.

A maintenance man, decked out in white, met me at the dock with a golf cart. I said I'd rather walk, and he trailed me to the pool house. I knew there was no doubt Gerey had prepped Brighthouse. A lawyer for a high-profile family and a political operative getting their messages aligned made perfect sense but never concerned me.

The maintenance man two steps behind me, I peeled off my jacket as soon as I stepped on the stone path. The island felt and looked different today. Maybe it was because no other officers were here. I slowed my pace, as there was something about this place. The mainland was visible, but the island was peacefully remote. If this guy wasn't babysitting me, I'd zig and zag my way to the pool house. As we stepped onto the pool deck, Gerey pulled open a slider and forced a smile.

"Good to see you, Detective."

Reflexively I said, "Likewise."

He lowered his voice. "I appreciate you coming alone. Gideon gets uncomfortable when there's too many people around."

"He got lucky; my partner's in court."

As we entered, Gideon Brighthouse rose out of a blue chair. Sockless, he was wearing a beige linen suit and red tee shirt that looked like paint had been splashed on it. Like the island, Gideon looked different today but still didn't offer his hand. Instead, he swept his arm toward a chair that looked like it was made of rope and sat back down.

I hadn't noticed the night the body was found, but there was a series of multimedia pieces that formed a band over the sliders. It heightened the effect that the glass doors were all connected. I'm no designer, but I'd never seen anything like it. It wasn't my style, but I gave whoever did it credit for originality.

"Mr. Brighthouse, I know this may be difficult, but I'd like to go over the day and night you found Mrs. Boggs in the main house."

Gideon nodded, picked up a Pellegrino water bottle and took a sip.

"Let's start right before you found the body. Where were you, and what were you doing?"

"As I said the other night, I was here, reading an article about Jasper Johns. I couldn't believe there was a mistake— in the name of one of his paintings. It's not a major work, but still." He shook his head, pausing. "I was sure they were wrong, but before I fired off a letter to them I wanted to be certain I was correct. I have a retrospective of his work. It's a wonderful book and the definitive reference on Johns."

There was no doubt he had rehearsed his recollection, but his manner of speaking was beginning to grate on me. I said, "I understand, go on."

"I went to the library to fact-check the Johns piece."

"Were you going to bring the book back here?"

"Absolutely not. I rarely take a book out, unless it's pure reading material. The library has proper reading surfaces. Some of the books in my collection . . . are quite large."

"Okay. On the way to the house, did you see or hear anything unusual?"

He shook his head. "No. It was just . . . another beautiful night."

"When you entered the house, you went straight to the library?"

"Yes."

"Now you're in the library, what happened next?"

"Anytime I go to the library, the first thing I do . . . is enjoy my one and only Pissarro, *Boulevard Montmartre at Night* . . . Impressionism at its best." He closed his eyes. "It's wonderful."

"I'm sure it is. What did you do next?"

"I took the Johns retrospective off the shelf."

"You said you heard water running and that was why you went into the kitchen. Is that right?"

"Why, yes. I was about to prove *Art Monthly* wrong . . . but before I had an opportunity to open the book, I heard what I believed to be water running, and went to check on it."

"Did you take the book with you?"

"Um, I believe so."

"When you entered the kitchen, what happened?"

"I was stunned and didn't comprehend . . . then I saw the blood. I tried to see if Marilyn was still alive . . . but she had no pulse." He looked around. "I think I may have panicked a bit . . . my chest was tightening, and with my history . . . I can't take chances."

"You said that you ran out. Is that accurate?"

He lowered his chin. "I'm afraid so."

"Were all the doors and windows closed?"

He shrugged. "I don't recall anything being open."

"I'm trying to get an accurate picture of your movements in the kitchen. You came in through the foyer, but the island blocked the view. As you went to shut the water off, is that when you saw your wife on the floor?"

"Yes."

"Okay. So, you bent over her and checked her pulse."

He nodded.

"Did you shut the water off?"

"I don't think so."

Gideon's cheeks seemed to redden a shade. *Was he lying? And why?* I said, "It's important, as the responding officer claims neither of the kitchen faucets was running."

Gerey said, "Perhaps it was Frank Flynn who shut the water off."

"Not according to what he told Detective Vargas. Flynn claimed not to have even been in the kitchen."

"I'm sure there is a practical explanation, Detective."

"Let's move on to the staff and any visitors during that day. Who was on the island?"

Gideon crossed his long legs and said, "No staff. The housekeepers and maintenance crew are off each Wednesday, but Marilyn had her friend John Barnet . . . over that afternoon."

This time there was no question, he blushed. "Is this John Barnet a mutual friend?"

"No. He's the proprietor of Barnet Wines in Waterside. Marilyn met him . . . when they did one of her charitable functions."

"What was the purpose of Mr. Barnet's visit?"

"It may have been in connection with an event."

"Mr. Brighthouse, was your wife having an affair with Mr. Barnet?"

Gerey said, "Detective, please. There's no reason to allude to—"

"Come on, Counselor. Mrs. Boggs was found dead in her own kitchen. That gives me the only reason that counts. Now, Mr. Brighthouse, please answer the question."

Gideon took a series of deep breaths as he studied his lap. "Yes . . . she was."

"How long had it been going on?"

Shrugging, Gideon said, "A year, year and a half, maybe longer."

"Was this the first affair your wife engaged in?"

Gerey rubbed his hands on his thighs as his client said, "No . . . there have been a couple of . . . others, but none that lasted as long."

"Do you have any reason to believe Mr. Barnet would want to harm Mrs. Boggs?"

"John Barnet thinks he's polished, and he is a leech, but I'm not qualified to evaluate him in regards to violence."

That surprised me. He didn't seem to want revenge or believe that Barnet did it. With all the transgressions, I could understand why he didn't care for his wife any longer. However, most men, this one included, wouldn't be able to resist the opportunity to deliver a dose of payback.

22

LUCA

"I don't like it, Vargas. How could he forget to tell us that this John Barnet was on the island the day his wife was killed?"

"I don't know, Frank. Maybe he was in shock that night. Don't forget, Gerey said Brighthouse sees a bunch of doctors."

"So, you're saying it wasn't an intentional omission?"

"No, I'm just saying this guy suffers from anxiety on normal days. Finding his wife murdered could've triggered shock or a mental shutdown of some kind."

"Morgan's gonna love this. First thing I should have done was interview the captain of the boat. Or the staff. For God's sake, what's wrong with me?"

"Let's move forward, Frank."

I lowered my chin and voice. "I think I've got chemo brain."

"Don't be so hard on yourself. Chemo brain—that's ridiculous."

"No, I mean it."

"Really? Okay, what about the fact that I didn't think of it either? So that makes two of us."

"It's not just this one thing, Mary Ann. I'm just not myself."

"It's in your head, Frank. You're an excellent detective, the best we've ever had down here."

"I'm serious, Mary Ann. I feel like I've been missing things I normally should see."

"Frank, you've been through a lot, and it's normal to feel like it took a toll on you. But I'm your partner, and I know you haven't missed a step. It's all in your head."

She was something, more than a partner, but I didn't believe a word she said. I sulked, and Vargas said, "As far as Morgan goes, he doesn't need to know all the little details." She came around her desk. "I'll tell him there's a chance we have another suspect, nothing more. Be back in ten."

"Thanks. While you go, I'll call Barnet and set up an interview."

Barnet was cooperative, as expected, and agreed to come in the next morning. He even waived his right to have an attorney present. Whether it was posturing or that he truly had nothing to fear would eventually surface.

I checked my phone again. Still no response from Kayla. I had sent her a text two days ago, and she never responded. What was going on? After debating whether to nudge her, I tapped out a text asking her if everything was okay.

MY MIND and my car were racing. Running late to see a house my Realtor said had possibilities, I couldn't stop considering approaches for tomorrow's interview of Barnet. Was this case going to take a turn? I always thought there were two types of murder cases: those where the killer was obvious and all we needed to do was collect evidence for the prosecution; and those puzzle types, often difficult, but that's where you earned your stripes. It was really satisfying to dig in, investigate a complex case, and arrest the killer. There were actually three types, but we detectives don't like to talk about those that go unsolved.

Making the turn from Airport onto Immokalee took a good five minutes, and Immokalee was backed up all the way to I-75. Buying something off this road might be a mistake I thought, as we crawled toward Walmart. Keeping my eyes off the clock was a strategy I used to help keep me from worrying about being late. As soon as I passed the Target Superstore, I realized taking Logan Boulevard would've avoided much of the traffic.

The entrance to Saturnia Falls had big boulders with tons of water rushing over them. I couldn't decide if it was over-done or not. Like most places in Naples, Saturnia had gotten its name from Italy, in this case inspired by a group of natural hot springs near the town of Saturnia.

After getting directions from the guard, I snaked my way to number 4290 Saturnia Grande Drive. A horde of kids were riding their bikes in the cul-de-sac about six houses away, confirmation that Saturnia was a full-time family type of community. The agent was walking down the driveway. I could see his comb-over. Didn't he get the memo that Bruce Willis made it okay to be bald?

He handed me the listing report and blabbed on about the community's amenities. I could hear a lot of road noise as he spoke, putting me on guard. I asked where it was coming from, and he said Logan Boulevard was just beyond the house, adding, "It's only busy this time of the day." I resisted telling him I was a detective and that the time-of-day statement rang my falsehood meter.

Since I was here, I took a quick look around. It had a nice floor plan, all open with high ceilings. It was a bit dated, but they had at least done the kitchen, though I wouldn't have chosen such a dark tile. The master bath had to be renovated, but the other bath and a half were livable. Going out to the lanai blew away any possible rationalization about the traffic. You could almost hear the people talking inside the cars as they went by.

The place was listed at four hundred grand, but I wouldn't buy if it was just a hundred. As I told Mr. Comb-over, I'd get back if I had any interest. My mind switched back to the Boggs case.

23

————

I'D KEPT JOHN BARNET WAITING FOR A GOOD TWENTY minutes and was surprised he hadn't taken a seat. He was tall, a good six feet three, and deeply tanned. He had a Van Dyke, was fit, and around fifty. Barnet was dressed in tan slacks and a jacket, with a light blue shirt. I wondered if he had put on a sport jacket for the interview and whether he was a lefty.

"Mr. Barnet, Detective Luca. Sorry to keep you waiting, but things are a bit busy given the investigation."

"I understand. If you need more time I'd be happy to come back."

I'm sure you would. "It's okay, let's get this over with. My office is just around the corner."

Barnet brushed the chair's seat and back with his left hand before sitting. A silver pin on his lapel reflected the light and I asked, "Not being nosy, Mr. Barnet, but the pin, what does it signify?"

He glanced at his lapel. "It's a sommelier pin. In my business, there's a ton of wannabes who just regurgitate the wine scores of critics. I differentiate myself, personalize the experience for our clients and make it more intimate with my opinions."

I guess telling him I chose a bottle based on its label and the price would blow a hole in his approach. "Sounds like a good strategy."

"I think so."

"It must be working if you can afford the Waterside rents."

He crossed his leg onto his knee and a red sock peeked out. "They don't make it easy."

"I bet. Look, I'd like to record this interview, if you don't object. Frankly, it makes it easier for me since my memory isn't what it used to be."

Barnet's eyes narrowed. "Record it?"

"If you're not comfortable, I won't then."

"It's okay, go ahead if you want."

Interviews and interrogations are chess games. You make a move to make your opponent respond in a way he otherwise wouldn't. Barnet agreed because he thought saying no would make him look bad. It works about seventy percent of the time. With the mic live, I covered the formalities and launched into the questioning before he had a chance to reconsider.

"You visited Mrs. Boggs on Keewaydin Island the day she was murdered."

Barnet shook his head. "Yeah, it's hard to believe what happened."

"I understand you provided Mrs. Boggs with wines and spirits for charitable events. Was that the reason you were there?"

"That's right. Marilyn was chairing the Catholic Charities event, and we went over a couple of items for it."

"How did you meet Mrs. Boggs?"

"My firm handles a fair number of events in the area, not just charitable ones, and if I recall correctly, we ran into each other at a United Way function."

"And the two of you just hit it off?"

Barnet stroked his Van Dyke and smirked. "We did, and as I'm sure you've heard, we were having an affair."

He thought he was building trust by admitting it, but he had to know that even in Naples there weren't enough charitable events to justify seeing Marilyn every Wednesday.

"And how long had this affair been going on?"

"A little over a year."

"How would you describe the, uh, temperature of the relationship?"

Barnet looked like he had bit into a lemon. "Temperature? You mean sex?"

"Did you encourage her to leave her husband?"

"No, I'd never do that. I don't want to have a broken marriage hanging over my head."

I smiled. "You're quite the nobleman."

"Very funny, but it's not like that. I come from a broken home, and it's no picnic."

"You were fine with just having an affair?"

"Look, we come from two very different worlds. I—I mean, we, we were just having a good time together. That's all it was."

"Just two consenting adults enjoying each other's company and nothing more."

"You could say that."

"The Boggs family is incredibly wealthy. It'd be some stroke of luck to marry into such a pile of cash, huh?"

"Money had nothing to do with it."

"You weren't upset that Mrs. Boggs wouldn't dump her husband and marry you?"

Barnet wagged his head. "Money aside, the last thing I need would be her as a wife. I've been married twice already and couldn't imagine doing it again."

"Not even into the Boggs family?"

"Nope."

"All right. Now, since you knew the deceased intimately," I couldn't stop a smile from breaking out, "do you know anyone who would want to harm her?"

Barnet grimaced. "Look, as I'm sure you'll find out if you don't already know, Marilyn was pretty insecure, despite all the money she had. And she could be arrogant and bossy, but she did nothing that would make anyone do something like this. She was a good woman. Geez, she really worked her tail off and helped so many people, it's hard to keep count."

"Marilyn Boggs had a high profile, possibly making her a target. Isn't there anyone that comes to mind?"

"Her husband, Gideon."

"Care to expound?"

"For starters, that day, the day she was . . . killed. Gideon came into the house while Marilyn and I were having a drink."

"Did he usually come when you were, er, visiting?"

"Never. But that day he did, and he seemed upset."

"Isn't that a natural reaction to seeing your wife with her lover?"

Barnet shrugged. "Something was different. I know him a little from when he worked for Senator White. We did a couple of functions for them. He was always, I don't know the right word, but scholarly is the closest I can think of. Gideon never got angry, was always levelheaded. I guess that's why the politicians liked him."

"And he wasn't on Wednesday?"

"No. He was crass. He referred to us having, I think it

was, a screw fest. It was out of character for him, and then he made some snide references about whether I was a sommelier. It was uncomfortable."

"I'll bet it was. How did the encounter break up?"

"I wanted to leave, but Marilyn was adamant that I stay, and she yelled at Gideon and he left."

"When she yelled, what did she say?"

"Nothing crazy, just telling him to calm down and that he was making a fool of himself."

"Nothing more? Anything that would set him off on a revenge rampage?"

"I don't think it was anything she said, but, like I said, he wasn't himself that afternoon."

"Is there anything else you can tell me?"

"Marilyn wanted to divorce him, but she didn't want to take the financial hit."

"They didn't have a prenuptial agreement?"

"Yeah, they did, but the trust had some clause that called for a penalty if you got divorced."

The word puritanical popped into my head. It sounded insane. Her father must have been some control freak, and he was still managing from the grave. It was an interesting twist.

24

LUCA

I hated valet parking, but the Ritz Carlton was not the place to park it yourself. The hotel's porte cochere was filled with so many Bentleys it looked like a dealer's lot. I'd heard the rental cars you got from the hotel's Hertz counter were nicer than at any other location, just another example of the coddling the Ritz did to makes its customers feel special.

A valet ran up and pulled my door open. I never tipped on the way in; this guy better not be looking for something.

"Hello, sir. Welcome to the Ritz Carlton. Are you checking in?"

"No, just meeting a friend for lunch."

"And your name?"

"Frank Luca."

He scribbled onto a ticket, tore it in half, and handed it to me.

"Enjoy your lunch, Mr. Luca."

A guy I thought I recognized from The Wine Loft was playing "I've Got You Under My Skin" on the lobby's grand piano. He was cooking. I checked the time, but I needed to get to the spa's lunch place. God forbid I kept Wesley Boggs waiting.

H2O was an informal, cafe-like restaurant on the second floor, right off of the Ritz's world-class spa. Maybe it was in my mind, or it might have been all the people traipsing around in robes, but the entire second floor had a feel that made me uncomfortable. How long had it been? The last massage I remembered was at a weekend bachelor party for my old partner JJ Cremora. It had to be at least fifteen years ago that we went to Atlantic City. Man, I still missed him like crazy, and the poor guy's been dead three years already.

I made a beeline for the door leading to a deck that had a covered dining area and a couple of soaking pools with chaise lounges. A pair of couples were seated at two of the tables. While I debated which table to take, a waitress approached.

"Welcome to H2O. May I seat you?"

"I'm meeting someone for lunch."

"Oh, perhaps they're here. What's the name?"

"Wesley Boggs."

Did this kid just straighten up a bit?

"Mr. Wesley is seated just over here."

I followed the kid around a wall of potted shrubbery that separated the cafe from the pool area. Seated at the head of a large table was Wesley Boggs. He was on the phone. He threw up a hand, flashing a paper-thin smile. Carrying fifteen to twenty pounds too much, his face was slightly puffy. Wesley didn't share his sister's frame or zest for exercise. His wet hair was graying and slicked back. I studied him as he finished his call; if I hadn't known he was loaded, I'd have never guessed it.

He got up and stuck his hand out. "Sorry. With what happened to Marilyn, there is just so much to deal with."

"I understand completely, Mr. Boggs. Please accept my condolences."

"Thank you, Mr. Luca."

Background information was what I was seeking, and I'd agreed with Gerey, who I'd half expected to be here, to keep it informal.

My tail had just hit the seat when the waitress appeared.

"Would you like something to drink?"

As I picked up the narrow menu, she said, "We're known for our juice drinks. They're healthy and nutritious."

"Sounds good, but I'll have an ice tea. Unsweetened."

Wesley said, "I've never understood why there isn't a view of the gulf up here. It's a shame."

The view of the pool areas looked pretty good to me. "That'd be a nice bonus."

Wesley surveyed the area and lowered his voice. "I understand you have some questions for me."

"Just a few, but let me start with the obvious one: Do you know of any reason someone would have done this?"

He wagged his head. "Not at all. Frankly, it seems surreal. Fortunately, though, Dad is not alive to suffer through this. It would have killed him. Marilyn was his favorite."

"I'm sorry your family has to go through all this."

"Thank you."

My ice tea was delivered and I said, "Your family is well known and thus could have been targeted. It's possible it had nothing to do with your sister. They could have been after the family in some way."

Wesley pulled his chin in. "We're really not a high-profile family, Mr. Luca. We lead quiet, private lives. Marilyn championed many charitable causes, taking active roles in many of them as well. However, that's not the family style. We do our philanthropic activities quietly. You know, Daddy always taught us to fly under the radar and to live beneath our means."

Really? Living on a private island while owning other homes ten minutes from each other and flying private jets qualifies as under the radar?

"So, no one comes to mind then?"

"Absolutely not."

"I'd like to talk about the trust that benefited your sister."

"The trust benefits all Boggs descendants."

"I understand that there are some unusual clauses in it that, for example, penalize someone if they get divorced."

"We don't consider them unusual. Daddy was vociferous in protecting the family. He didn't want marriage to be a casual endeavor, which I agree with. He wanted to be sure full consideration was given, and if you found out you made a mistake there would be consequences."

These people were different, no doubt. "Prohibiting divorce could lock people like Marilyn in a marriage she'd rather not be in."

Wesley blinked twice. "It's not prohibited. You can get divorced if you wish. You'll just have a reduction in benefits."

"May I ask how much?"

"The trust is a private document. I don't believe I should be disclosing that information."

"Fair enough. Did you know that your sister was having an affair?"

He nodded. "We warned her on several occasions to be discreet."

"In a situation like this, with Marilyn deceased, what happens to Gideon?"

He tilted his head.

"Does he still, as you say, benefit from the trust?"

"There are clauses that provide for almost every situation, but, yes, he still benefits, albeit at a reduced amount."

"Do you believe that your brother-in-law was involved?"

"I've thought about the possibility, but Gideon isn't ambitious, at least not since he had heart troubles. I couldn't envision it, certainly not him personally doing it."

I took a sip of my iced tea, thanked him for his time, and left.

Disappointed Wesley didn't point the finger at Gideon, I walked to the valet station. I was digging in my pocket for the ticket when the kid behind the podium said, "Mr. Luca, how was your lunch?"

How the heck do these guys remember?

25

LUCA

I buttoned up my suit jacket as I walked the corridor to the autopsy suite. What a terrible qualifier for a room where they cut bodies up. Why not something simple, like autopsy room? I jammed my hands into my pants pockets. It's easy to understand why the autopsy room has to be cold, but how anyone works anywhere in the building without a parka on is a mystery to me.

The light over the door was off and a peer in the door's window confirmed the room was empty. Was it the fact I wouldn't have to see another body dissection, or that I wouldn't have to stand in a room that was twenty degrees colder than the hallway that made me smile?

Wearing a gray cardigan and headphones, the medical examiner was behind his desk, tapping on a keyboard.

"Hey, Doc!"

He looked up at me and paused his player.

"Got a few minutes to fill me in on the Marilyn Boggs autopsy?"

Setting down the headphones, he said, "Come on in, Frank. I'm just finishing the report now."

"I wanted to make it but got hung up. How'd it go?"

"No surprises. A deep stab wound to the thorax, clipping the aorta, which led to a bleed out. The wound was inflicted by a knife matching the one found on the scene. Trace elements of the victim's blood were found on the knife."

"It was wiped clean of prints, though?"

"As far as I understand, but you'd have to check with forensics."

"Could you speculate on the physical size of the killer?"

"The angle of the entry wound supports an attacker, left handed I believe, in the six feet to six feet six range. However, it's really dependent on the arm's length and whether the victim was leaning away from her attacker."

"Um, anything under the fingernails?"

"Nothing. She had a head bruise, just under the dome, from striking her head on the edge of the counter as she lost consciousness. The victim's right wrist is bruised, but that likely occurred trying to break her fall."

I nodded as he continued.

"Stomach contents didn't reveal anything other than some wine and a cracker or bread-like food. Alcohol blood level a tad under .09. With her weight, the victim probably had two glasses of wine."

"How impaired would she have been?"

"Depends on her tolerance, but probably overly relaxed, depth and peripheral vision impacted slightly."

"Could've contributed to an inability to detect an attack?"

"Difficult to say for sure, but a lag in reaction time is likely."

"Anything else you can tell me?"

"The victim had a hysterectomy about five to seven years ago."

That didn't seem to mean anything but prompted me to ask, "Any signs of sexual activity?"

"None. I'd estimate about five days since the last intercourse."

HEADING NORTH AS I DEFROSTED, I was pleased Goodlette Frank Road was empty. Crossing Golden Gate, Vargas returned my call.

"Hi Frank. Anything from the autopsy?"

"Nah, didn't learn anything. She died from the knife wound, and it matches the one at the scene. Forensics said the knife was definitely wiped clean of prints."

"Really?"

"You had to expect it. No killer would leave it behind unless they did."

"But leaving it behind to begin with is a risk."

"No doubt."

"Any clues to how it went down?"

"No signs of a real struggle. She seems to have been quickly overpowered. Stab wound indicates a lefty, a tall one, at least six feet. The knife wound severed her aorta. She bled out quickly, a minute or two."

"Any toxicology reports yet?"

"Not a full panel, but blood tests indicate a low level of alcohol that raises a question."

"How so?"

"Doc said her alcohol levels were the equivalent of two glasses of wine or so."

"And?"

"The pinot bottle at the scene had only a quarter left in it, and there was just one glass out, and it was clean. She couldn't have drank it alone. So, whoever was there took their glass."

"Or she was drinking, or going to drink, from a bottle that was already open."

"I'm betting Marilyn wasn't a leftovers type of girl."

"Maybe, but you'd be surprised; even the wealthy like to save money."

"I don't doubt that, but remember, she was playing around with Barnet, an expert on wine. He would've rubbed off on her."

"You're going to see him. Why don't you just ask?"

"Not yet. If he's involved in some way, I'll need to hold back a thing or three."

"Another Luca proverb?"

"I'd like to take credit, but that was my old partner's saying. I'll see you when I get back from Waterside."

SWIRLING A GLASS, Barnet was in the cave at the back of the store. There were two women at the table with him. I edged a few steps closer, picking up a bottle of Barolo as a decoy. Barnet tipped his glass on its side and rolled it back and forth with his palm. The women at the table glanced at each other and broke into smiles. Barnet picked the glass back up and stuck his nose deeply in it. He closed his eyes and his chest expanded. Releasing air, he raised the glass to his lips and took a sip. He moved his lips around and his Adam's apple bobbed.

Nodding his head, Barnet set the glass down and poured the women wine. The women fingered the glasses, shifting them side to side, laughing as a splash jumped out of a glass.

Barnet dabbed the table with a napkin and said, "I think it's wonderful, a great mouth feel, good acidity. It's a very balanced wine. I'm interested to hear what you think."

The two women sipped and nodded at each other.

"I like it. It's smooth, like you said."

"Yeah, no hard edges. What foods do you recommend with it, John?"

"That's one of the things I love about this particular wine. It's so versatile. Chicken, veal, and pork will pair well with it."

"What's the price of a case?"

"It's a great value. I think the *Wine Spectator* featured it as one of their better buys a month or two ago."

"Oh, wow."

"It's eighty-nine ninety-five a bottle and selling quicker than I anticipated. I think we have only three cases left. Shall I have Bridgette write up a case for each of you?"

Did he just say ninety dollars a bottle? Didn't these people ever hear of Costco? I put the Barolo back on the rack as the women agreed to a case each. Was that considered a soft or a hard sell?

Barnet picked up the bottle and was topping off their glasses when I stepped into the cave.

One of the women said, "Oh, John, it looks like the wine-maker from Bordeaux is here."

Barnet spun around, and the color drained out of his face. "Oh, hi. I'll be right with you." He turned back to his guests. "It's not Francois, but I've got to go. I'm sure you'll enjoy the wine, ladies. Thanks for stopping in."

He got up from the table and shook my hand. "Let's go to my office."

Barnet closed the door and slid behind his desk. He

moved a large bottle, which had been signed in gold, to a corner as I settled into a chair.

"I didn't know you were coming by, Detective."

"I was in the area and had a couple of questions for you. Thought it would be easier than having you come down."

"Oh. Thanks for saving me a trip."

"No problem. I gotta say, you did a nice sales job on them."

Barnet stroked his Van Dyke and wagged a finger. "I don't consider it sales. It's really all about introducing and educating. I consider it important—no, make that critical—to move people's perception of wine from simply a beverage to an experience. Paint a story of the vineyards, the winery, and the winemaker for them so they can be transported when they drink a wine. It makes the cost factor irrelevant, as it should be."

Transported? He keeps talking like that, he's going to be transported to an asylum.

"Got it. As I said, there's a couple of questions concerning Marilyn Boggs, so let's get to it, shall we?"

Barnet sank back and nodded.

"When you visited with her on the afternoon of her death, did you have any wine or alcoholic drinks of any kind?"

"Marilyn was really beginning to understand and enjoy wine. She especially liked a glass of French Viognier during the afternoon, and every Wednesday I'd bring a different producer over to sample. It was educational. I was trying to get her to discover the different ways the soil and microclimates of each vineyard affect the wine."

Fun? That sounded like work to me. "How much did she drink that day?"

"I think she may have had two glasses."

"Did she like other types of wine?"

Barnet furrowed his brow. "She enjoyed Sauvignon Blanc from the Loire Valley and French chardonnays."

"So, just white wine?"

"Mostly. I was trying to introduce her to Barolo and the wines of Bordeaux, but I guess she had her limits."

"She didn't like Chianti or pinot noir?"

He shook his head. "Occasionally she'd drink pinot," he laughed, "but that might have been because I kept telling her the best wines in the world, in my opinion, were from Burgundy."

"Burgundy?"

"The reds from Burgundy, France, are made from pinot noir grapes. They're less fruit forward and more complex than those from California."

"Sounds interesting. I'll have to try some."

"I'll pick out one for you to try when you leave. It'll be on me."

"Thanks, but I can't accept a gift. I'll pay for it but keep it under thirty bucks."

"I have a couple in mind."

"Okay. How would you describe the stage your relationship with Marilyn Boggs was in?"

"What do you mean?"

"The affair was going for a pretty long time. Was the fire still there?"

"Oh, at the beginning it was kinda like a high school fling." He flashed a smile. "But things settled down into a nice routine."

"Routine? Sounds boring to me."

"I didn't mean to imply that it was boring. Just that when we first started . . . to . . . to get together, we looked for every opportunity we could. That's why I said it was like high school. But then we fell into a schedule, like every Wednesday afternoon and most Friday nights."

"Who was more, shall we say, enthusiastic?"

"We both looked forward to seeing each other, but, you gotta remember, I'm running a business, and it takes a lot of my time, while Marilyn, well, she had a lot of time on her hands."

"A friend of hers said she thought the relationship was coming to an end."

"No, that's not true."

"But it had cooled down?"

"As I said, things settled down."

"Did the two of you fight often?"

"I wouldn't use the word fight, Detective. Did we disagree at times? Sure, what couple doesn't?"

"It seems that something was bothering Mrs. Boggs in the weeks leading to her murder. Do you have any idea what was on her mind?"

Barnet stroked his Van Dyke. "I think it may have something to do with the situation with her husband."

"You mean the affair you were having?"

"No, no. The marriage was over. It had nothing to do with me. You probably know she had an affair or two before we met. She really wanted a divorce from him, but there were some things in the trust she lives off that would penalize her."

Barnet knew about the details of the trust? "That's interesting. What was she going to do?"

He shifted in his chair. "She was probably kidding, but she said something about having him disappear."

"You mean by paying him off to disappear?"

"Could be, but I understood it as, you know, having him killed."

"Do you think Marilyn Boggs would arrange for the murder of her husband?"

"I know it sounds crazy, but I'm telling you that's what she said."

I was processing the thought when Barnet added, "You have to remember, the Boggs are a very powerful family."

26

LUCA

"I DON'T LIKE IT, VARGAS. WHY THE HELL DIDN'T HE TELL us? This Gideon guy, he's our number one right now."

"Maybe he was embarrassed, Frank. It's not so easy to tell somebody, especially a man, that your wife was cheating on you, no less in the poor guy's own house."

"I'm glad I keep you around, Vargas. You make a good point every now and then."

Vargas crumpled paper into a ball and tossed it at me.

"You're a piece of work. How long you going to make him stew?"

"Another twenty or thirty minutes."

"You sure about that? This guy gets anxious fast, and no sense having Gerey pissed at us."

"Wow." I got up. "Two good points in one day. Let's have our chat with Gideon."

Before we went into interrogation room two, we checked on the video feed coming from the room. Gideon was swiveling his head like he was watching a tennis match and pinching his shirt away from his chest every five seconds.

"We're sorry to keep you waiting, Mr. Brighthouse. The captain called us in on another case."

"Okay." He took a deep breath. "Okay."

"You remember my partner, Detective Vargas?"

He nodded and came halfway out of his chair when Mary Ann said, "It's okay, sit. Would you like something to drink?"

"Uh, no. I'm . . . okay."

After I dictated the formalities of the interview, I said, "We asked you down here because both your original statement on the night of your wife's murder and your statement in a subsequent interview puzzled us."

Gideon rubbed his hands on his thigh. "How? I . . . I didn't mean to confuse anyone. You, you can be sure, it certainly wasn't intentional."

"How come you failed to tell us that you confronted your wife and John Barnet on the very afternoon of the day she was found dead?"

Gideon's shoulders sagged. "I . . . I don't know."

Vargas asked, "Did you find it embarrassing to talk about?"

"No."

This guy was nuts. "No? Your wife is having an affair and meeting her lover at your house, and that didn't bother you?"

"If you must know, it wasn't the first one. May I have a glass of water?"

Vargas hit the intercom as Gideon squirmed like a six-year-old waiting to get into an amusement park.

"There's no need to get unsettled, Mr. Brighthouse, just answer the questions we have with honest answers and everything will be fine."

Gideon's head bobbed as the door swung open and a bottle of water was handed off to him. He took it with his left hand, raising the bottle too quickly, and drops of water darkened his tan shirt. He dabbed at the corner of his mouth, mumbling a thank you.

"How many affairs did your wife engage in?"

"Four."

"When did this all start?"

"I . . . I . . . it was sometime after my heart attack."

Vargas asked, "While you were recuperating?"

Gideon nodded.

I said, "I can tell you, that would have upset me, especially if I was recovering. Man, that's hitting under the belt as far as I'm concerned. Pissed off would be an understatement."

Gideon took a sip of water but remained silent.

I said, "John Barnet said you were angry that afternoon, that you were making comments and Marilyn told you to calm down. Is that what transpired?"

"Was I happy? No, but I'd learned to . . . live with the situation. My therapist helped me to realize how important art is to me . . . it makes me happy . . . and I'm at peace on Keewaydin. Uh, how much longer will this take? I need to get back."

"Did you argue with Marilyn when Barnet left the island?"

"We've never really argued . . . Marilyn . . . she wasn't the type, she had a lot of control."

"And how about you?"

"I have all the human frailties."

Interesting way of putting it, I'd have to remember that when I screwed up.

Vargas said, "Given the uncomfortable circumstances in your marriage, didn't you want to get divorced?"

"Yes, but Marilyn resisted the . . ."

I said, "So you killed her."

"No, no, I didn't . . . I had no reason to."

"Look Gideon, we know all about the trust and how Marilyn would suffer financially if she got a divorce. The only way out for you was to kill her."

"That's completely untrue. In fact, she wanted to get divorced. She took me by surprise the other day."

"Really? You expect us to believe that?"

"But, but it's true . . . she said it . . . about two weeks ago."

"That's very convenient."

"You don't . . . understand. She was being vin . . . vindictive. Wanted me to leave." Gideon jumped out of his seat. "I gotta go. I can't stay."

I looked at Vargas, who said, "Let him go, Frank. It looks like he's having a panic attack."

"What if he's faking it?"

"He might be, but if he has another heart attack, this room won't be able to hold all of his lawyers."

ON THE WAY TO look at a new listing in Pelican Marsh, I still felt like Gideon had faked his attack. Revealing that we knew he'd confronted his wife and her boyfriend, along with our awareness of the penalty facing both of them for divorce, had put him on the spot. Then he goes and says that his wife agreed to divorce him? Unless she had filed, there was no way to check it. It was nothing more than hearsay, and I didn't buy it. Gerey said he had no knowledge but would check with a couple of divorce lawyers in the county that served the wealthy.

Getting a look at the trust documents and especially the prenuptial agreement could provide a concrete motive.

Problem was, the DA was hesitant about asking a judge to sign an order. Said he didn't believe we had enough and that he was concerned with intruding on the family's privacy. Even when I suggested a gag order and limiting access to the documents to him and me, he didn't change his attitude.

I had forgotten how nice the Pelican Marsh entrance fountain was. The circular fountain threw up mountains of dense white water and offset the guardhouse, which I thought was one of the nicer ones in town.

The listing was in Grand Isles, a community of courtyard homes. I wasn't a big fan of courtyard homes, but when I started the house hunt I was considering getting a dog, and a courtyard made sense. It was stupid and impulsive to consider a pet just because Kayla loved dogs. I had been thinking and dreaming like a seventeen-year-old. How the hell did I let what amounted to two dates with Kayla, influence my thinking? She was different, and I had high hopes, but the reality was there were miles of ground to cover if the relationship was to go anywhere, and it wasn't looking good now.

The home had more square footage than I wanted, and needed work, which I wasn't sure I was up to. The Realtor said it was the best buy in the Marsh, so here I was.

There were lakes on either side of the street, but this house was the first one on the left after the gate. I started to reconsider the location and pet thing and decided to leave. The Realtor hadn't arrived yet, so I made a U-turn and left. I called the agent and told her an emergency at the sheriff's office made it impossible for me to make the showing.

27

GIDEON BRIGHTHOUSE

THE WALL BEHIND THE DETECTIVES WAS MOVING CLOSER AND there were white spots moving over their faces. I couldn't stay here; the tightness in my chest was surging, and it could be a heart attack coming. I tried to get up but was glued to the seat. My peripheral vision was shrinking so fast I wouldn't be able to find the door. I had to go. They can't force me to stay. I'm going to die here.

Grabbing the edge of the table, I pried myself out of the chair. "I gotta go. I can't stay."

Clutching the doorknob with trembling hands, I escaped into the hallway. It was a maze. As a flash of heat scooted up my spine, I saw a glass door leading to the parking lot and ran. The open space slowed my breathing down, but a ball of fire in my gut erupted, forcing me to bend over and vomit.

NAVIGATING THROUGH GORDON PASS CHANNEL, we crossed the entrance to Dollar Bay and Keewaydin came into view. Every pore on my body sprung open, leaking the tension that had knotted me up. As my breathing returned to normal, I had trouble staying awake and stood up, putting my face into the breeze. As the boat maneuvered into a slip, I jumped off before the captain finished edging closer.

I jogged off the dock and took a couple of deep breaths, sucking in the island's serenity. Keewaydin delivered peace better than a dozen Valiums. My phone rang. Gerey wanted to know how the interview went. I told him the police were insinuating that I was involved in Marilyn's murder. Gerey promised to speak with them and to warn them against libeling me.

His assurance felt good but only lasted about ten steps. Gerey represented the Boggs family. I was a distant number two at best. He was probably told to keep an eye on me by Paul, the brother who was as controlling as the old man. I was never one of the family and rarely saw them, excepting Christmas and the annual shareholder meetings.

There was an interesting period when the relationship seemed to thaw a bit. Marilyn had bragged about how I'd virtually discovered Tracey Emin and that the six pieces of hers we had bought had increased twentyfold in a year. The brothers were shrewdly skeptical, telling both of us that I'd gotten lucky but asking the family office, under the guise of having adequate insurance, for an appraisal. When the appraisal came in at close to thirty times what we'd paid, they did a dizzying reversal

They were so transparent when they approached me about art that it was laughable, but I didn't care. They wanted to build a collection quietly and quickly. I spent the better part of eighteen months visiting new, up-and-coming artists. It was the most fun I'd had since the early days of collecting. I'd done very well for them, picking up eight sculptures by

Matthew Barney and a half-dozen paintings by Elizabeth Peyton before anyone knew who the artists were.

Notwithstanding the help I provided, the brothers remained distant and ungrateful. After the budget they had set aside was spent, and despite the increase in value, I was persona non grata. I went into a funk. Marilyn thought I was insulted, but what gave me the blues was being unable to see the pieces I curated. It was the ultimate nightmare scenario. The brothers treated the collection like an investment and stored it in a Boston warehouse. When I told Marilyn how I felt, she laughed at me, and when I tried to explain to her how much it meant to me, she made a demeaning comment that they were just decorative items.

The pool house was freezing. I raised the thermostat and lowered myself onto the couch, reminding myself it was all about the wealth for the Boggs. I slid into sleep, wondering if the family would use its weight to jail me for Marilyn's death.

28

LUCA

THE STATION WAS BUZZING WITH ACTIVITY. MY OFFICE WAS next door to the area where roll call was held, and Sergeant Gesso's baritone voice was tough to block out. Needing to think, I closed the door to my office and ran through my messages. I had to treat as real what Barnet told us about Marilyn doing away with her husband. The family was powerful and had unlimited financial resources. That combo, juiced by a strong dose of arrogant intelligence, had doomed countless others who believed they could mastermind a crime and get away with it.

Did Gideon discover a plot to get rid of him and respond by killing his wife? Could the case be that twisted? It was an irrational response, but most murders were. How would he have learned about it? Marilyn could have let it slip, or maybe she taunted him with the threat? The family was tight-lipped and guarded but, by all accounts, Marilyn's affairs were well outside the lines of the family's behavior. She didn't seem to use any discretion. Plenty of people, including Gideon, knew about her escapades. It was possible she threatened him and he reacted.

If he had come to the police with an oral threat, would we have treated it as real? No way. Unless he had hardcore proof, it would have been dismissed as domestic chatter, especially given the players involved.

Vargas opened the door. "It's safe, roll call is over."

"Maybe Morgan will tell him to tone it down."

"I think he's gotten louder, trying to impress him."

"The Barnet revelation that Marilyn wanted to get rid of her husband makes gaining access to the trust even more important."

"How so? Her brother already acknowledged she'd be penalized for divorcing."

"Yeah, but one, we don't know by how much, and two, we don't know what we don't know. Who knows what else is in there? Even if there wasn't a plan to kill Gideon, we could learn a lot from the documents. Remember, greed is the most powerful motivator for murder. You ask me, this one's all about the money."

"What's that, two Luca parables today?"

"You don't agree?"

"You're probably right, but I'm not giving up on the jilted lover angle."

"I think we can make a case for a subpoena of Gideon's phone and computer records. It's supported by either the money or the being jilted motives."

———

VARGAS CAME BACK from the second floor and gave a thumbs-down.

"Tell me you're kidding, Mary Ann."

She shook her head.

"This is crazy. How the hell can they deny the request?"

"You forget who we're talking about, Frank?"

"You think Gerey got to the DA?"

"No, they don't need to. The name alone intimidates. They're gonna be super careful. The last thing they need is bad publicity going after a grieving husband."

"It's for their benefit, for crying out loud."

"If it's any consolation, he said—"

I jumped out of my chair. "We got it backward. We need to get inside the trust first."

"How we going to do that? Didn't her brother Wesley say no? If we can't get Gideon's communications, how we going get them to subpoena a private document?"

"Gerey's going to give us access to it."

"What? Are you sure?"

I picked up the phone and made an appointment to see the Boggs family attorney.

WHITE, Gerey and Blackburn occupied a two-story, white stucco building just north of Golden Gate. Tucked away in the left-hand corner of a small parking lot that served two other buildings, you needed a microscope to see their sign. Two late-model Mercedes framed the single door into the offices, which felt more like a home than a law firm.

Gerey was seated in a far corner, signing documents at a round table when we entered. He penned a couple more before rising to greet us, shooing away a secretary who had started toward us. As we shook hands, he said, "Let's step into my office."

Gerey's office was done in a dark-paneled wood I thought was walnut. Heavy drapes shut out most of the light. Gerey slid behind an oversized desk that anchored the room, and Vargas and I took seats in green leather-wing chairs.

"How can I help you, Detectives?"

I said, "We're pursuing a couple of avenues and believe the trust may hold clues to who murdered Mrs. Boggs."

A smirk formed on Gerey's lips. "Clues? Please don't tell me the sheriff's department believes that a trust, drawn up decades ago, contains information on the murderer?"

"Let me be more specific. We already know from Wesley Boggs, among others, that the trust contained clauses that would penalize Marilyn Boggs for getting a divorce."

Cobra-like, Gerey looked straight at me but said nothing.

I said, "We'd like to get a clearer picture of what financial incentives are in the trust."

"The trust is a private document and is unrelated to the tragic murder of one of its beneficiaries. The family will never permit it to be made public."

Vargas said, "We understand and respect the family's privacy."

"Well, that's it then. I'm glad we agree on that."

I said, "Hold on. Let me be direct, and I apologize in advance if I cross any lines."

Gerey clasped the arms of his chair and said, "If you wish to, go ahead."

"Rather than viewing our access as an invasion of privacy, and it would be limited to just my partner and me with you in the room, think of it as a possible windfall."

"Windfall? Detective Luca, you promised to be direct."

"If we find something in the trust or otherwise that points responsibility for the murder to Gideon Brighthouse, I'm sure any inheritance he would be entitled to would be stripped away, leaving the money to the rest of the family."

Gerey silently steepled his hands.

Vargas said, "Either way, it would help clarify Gideon Brighthouse as either a suspect or clear him. I'm sure the family would like to quiet the rumors and suspicions that are dragging the them through the mud."

I said, "We have no interest in seeing the entire document, just the parts that involve Marilyn, Gideon, and their marriage."

Gerey rolled his tongue over his teeth. "The sooner we clarify if Mr. Brighthouse has a role other than as a grieving husband, the better. The family needs closure, and I'll agree to allow you access. However, access will be strictly limited to prenuptial references, divorce repercussions, and rights in the event of spousal death."

I said, "That's fine. It's all we're interested in seeing."

"I will not allow any copying. However, you may take notes, but they'll be prohibited from publication. Is that understood?"

Man, would I like to ram a subpoena up this guy's ass.

Vargas said, "That's fine. We appreciate the cooperation, Mr. Gerey."

Gerey nodded and picked up the phone. "Clara, please phone Mrs. Whitestone. Tell her something urgent has come up and reschedule her appointment for an opening next week."

He hung up and rose. "I suggest you come back in an hour. I'll have a nondisclosure agreement drafted for your signature, and it'll give me time to scrutinize the documents to identify the relevant sections."

GEREY SHOWED us into a conference room with an oval-shaped, dark walnut table. Sitting in the middle was a four-inch thick white binder emblazoned with Boggs Family in black. My thoughts went from what was in it to how much Gerey charged to put it together.

Three neon colored Post-it notes hung just past the cover. Vargas and I sat in front of the binder and Gerey slid it between us, opening it to a page with a pink Post-it. It was about a quarter of the way into the sheath of documents.

"Section thirteen B. The Boggs prenuptial agreement. You should be aware that in section eleven C, I believe, entrance into this prenuptial is a prerequisite for participation in the trust."

Vargas asked, "Everybody has the same prenuptial?"

"For those who wish to marry, yes. Any family member who wishes to benefit from the trust must execute this exact agreement. No deviations are permitted."

There was a plastic separator just a few pages down. I flipped to it and said, "The prenup section is only three pages long?"

"Indeed. Short and to the point. As will become clear to you, Martin Boggs frowned on divorce. You'll find the section on separations and divorce concise as well."

Vargas took her moleskin out and jotted down the essentials. At the time of a court-approved divorce, a one-time payment of one hundred thousand dollars would be made, along with an annual stipend of forty thousand dollars to spouses of beneficiaries. Assets acquired during the marriage would remain under the control and ownership of the Boggs family trust.

It sounded tough, but I could see the old man's point in keeping the gold diggers away. I wondered what kind of money Gideon had when they got married. He was in politics, so if he was like most politicians, he would have found a way to accumulate a hefty sum.

I flipped to the middle of the binder where a lime green Post-it marked Section 27. It was all of five pages. Vargas started jotting notes, but I had to read the legalese twice to get the picture; if a beneficiary got divorced, their benefits would be reduced by twenty-five percent. That was a hell of a price to pay to get out of a marriage. I was already trying to figure what that meant in dollars.

The last section we got a peek at was marked by a blue sticky and was almost the last part of the trust. It dealt with the deaths of beneficiaries. There were parts of the section that were paper-clipped together, and when I asked, Gerey told us they dealt with the unmarried, children, and infants. Boy, these guys had everything covered.

It took a few minutes of looking, but the number was worth the hunt. A spouse of a beneficiary who died was entitled to twenty million dollars.

I asked, "Am I reading this correctly? Someone like Gideon would get twenty million?"

"Yes."

"Boy, with these numbers it's a wonder the trust doesn't run out of money."

Gerey said, "Life insurance policies on each beneficiary more than cover the spousal entitlement."

That was interesting. The trust made money on the death of Marilyn Boggs. I needed to know how much life insurance there was and how much money was sitting in the trust to see if it amounted to a motivator for the current and future beneficiaries, which meant her brothers and their offspring. If they made even ten million from the life insurance payout but the trust was a billion, it was a speck of sand.

"What are the total assets of the trust?"

"That is private and outside of the scope of our agreement."

"Was the trust struggling to keep supporting its beneficiaries?"

Gerey stood up. "I believe we've been more than cooperative, Detective Luca. I'll have to conclude this meeting."

It was an abrupt ending, and I wondered if we'd hit a nerve.

29

LUCA

CAPITAL PAWN WAS HOUSED IN A STAND-ALONE WHITE building that had one of those roofs with a lot of angles. For some reason, that roof style always reminded me of Indonesia, even though I'd never been there. Capital Pawn had a bunch of places, but this one was in Lehigh Acres, on Homestead Road.

It was across the street from the Lee County Sheriff's office, and that was why it wasn't offered stolen goods too often.

It was a big shop, a mini-department store. The right-hand side was divided into sections for electronics, musical instruments, and tools. To the left were appliances, sporting goods, and firearms, where a customer was shouldering a rifle. There were about thirty rifles and at least as many pistols hanging on the wall. Though I'd been a Floridian for a couple of years, I couldn't get used to all the places firearms were offered for sale.

Dead center, signaling where Capital made its money, was a series of glass cabinets rivaling Macy's jewelry department.

Two men were behind the counter, one with a suit and tie. I introduced myself and the suit took over, quickly escorting me to his office.

"You know as soon as we received the alert from Collier we made sure the staff was tuned into what was going on."

"We appreciate the cooperation."

"Capital prides itself on being a good citizen."

"You said you had video?"

He picked up a disk that was sitting in the center of his desk and waved it. "Every one of our stores is outfitted to document sellers and the merchandise they have. It eliminates a lot of headaches when and if they want to buy back what they brought in."

"I'd like to see that footage before I seize it."

He popped the disk in and fast-forwarded to a time stamp of 6:50 p.m. The quality of the video was much better than I expected. A tall man, who looked Hispanic, walked up to the counter and spoke with a woman salesperson.

I said, "Freeze that. Who is the lady?"

"Sally Kerchow."

"Is she here today?"

He shook his head. "Sorry, she's off today."

"I'd like her contact details. She may have to testify. Let it roll."

The man in the video pulled a small pouch from his front pocket and laid it on the counter. He used his left hand. Sally opened the pouch and took out a cocktail ring. She held the ring between her thumb and forefinger and examined it. She said something to the man and pulled out a loupe, put it to her eye and brought the ring up to it. After inspecting the ring, she put it back in the pouch. They had a brief discussion. The man pocketed the pouch and departed.

"What did she say to him?"

"Sally knows her stuff. She used to work in the jewelry department at Saks. She recognized the ring right away. It wasn't your normal cocktail ring. The stones were out-sized, and the setting was definitely custom. She told him they had too much inventory at the time and to come back next month."

"Did she or anyone recognize who he was? Was he here before?"

"Though we have a lot of repeat customers, no one knew him."

"You showed this to everyone who works here?"

"Of course."

"If we can't ID this guy, I might be asking you to have your other stores take a look at this video."

IT TOOK our video guys less than half an hour to produce five clear photos of the man looking to pawn what was confirmed as Marilyn's stolen ring. I held the photos like a hand of cards. No one down in robbery could place the face, which puzzled me. No way this was a first dance for him. I get the isolation part if you were committing a robbery for the first time, but on an island? And even though the Boggs had zero security on Keewaydin, unless you knew that, you'd have to assume a high-end home like theirs would have the best.

So, what was it? Was it a murder by hire? Paid for in jewelry? Or an inside job of some kind? Either way, we had to move carefully. We couldn't risk letting anyone know we had a line on the thief and possible murderer.

As soon as Vargas got back, I'd send her out to

Keewaydin since she had developed a bit of a rapport with the housekeeper. With any luck, the maid would identify the man who tried to fence the cocktail ring. If she couldn't, we'd have to broaden the search by publishing pictures, sacrificing an element of surprise.

30

LUCA

RAUL SANCHEZ WAS THIRTY-SEVEN YEARS OLD AND LIVED A couple of miles from the casino in Immokalee. He'd come to the States from Mexico about six years ago and had a legitimate green card. Sanchez, whose driver's license said he was six feet, didn't have a record in the States and had worked for the Boggs for just under two years. According to Shell, the housekeeper, he was recommended by the landscaping contractor when the pool was renovated.

Standing outside interrogation room three, I found myself wishing we had more intelligence on Sanchez. It'd been two days since we asked the Mexican Federal Police for anything on him, but they still hadn't responded. All we had was him trying to fence a cocktail ring. Maybe I should have waited or asked the State Department to make inquiries.

It would be nice to have Vargas help interview Sanchez. I sent her a text, but she didn't reply. She was probably still stuck in court.

I found myself questioning my instincts again, something I never did before I got hit with cancer. Self-doubt, both physical and mental, had seeped into my core. It felt like I'd made a mistake again, but now I didn't have much of a choice; Sanchez was stewing behind the door.

Checking again, there still wasn't a message from Vargas. I grabbed the knob and opened the door. Sanchez was sitting like a schoolboy at the steel table. He swung his head toward me, revealing a crude tattoo on his neck. The rendering of a snake screamed jailhouse and bolstered me. Maybe I wasn't losing it after all.

"I'm Detective Luca. I'm heading the investigation into the Marilyn Boggs murder." I sat across from him and centered my folder.

"It's a shame what happened to her. She was a nice lady."

He had less of an accent than the lady at the pawn shop had said. "How long have you been working on Keewaydin?"

"About two years. I got the job when I was working with Gonzalvo Landscaping. We was doing the pool for them."

"What are your duties there?"

"Well, to be honest, just about anything, you know, that needs to be done: taking care of the landscaping and beach areas, keeping up with things like painting and minor repairs. There's always stuff that needs to be done."

"With the size of that place, just changing the light bulbs would keep someone busy."

"Those are some high ceilings. I need to take a twelve-footer to reach the high hats."

"How many maintenance people are there?"

"There's me, Mr. Pena, he's the manager, Pedro, and Emilio."

"So, four full-timers?"

"Yeah, we get it all done. But sometimes we gotta bring in help when it's a big job, like when we upgraded the dock."

"Has there been a need recently to bring any outside help in?"

"Last time, I think was for the roof on the main house. A couple of panels were, like, rusting. They were defective or something."

"When was that?"

"Uh, maybe five, six months ago."

"Do you know anyone who might have wanted to harm Mrs. Boggs?"

He shook his head. "No, she was nice lady."

"That's what they tell us. She wore a lot of jewelry, I hear."

His Adam's apple bobbed as he shrugged.

"Did you ever work inside the main house?"

He shook his head. "No, I worked mostly on the landscaping."

"Didn't you say you used a big ladder to change the light bulbs?"

His shoulders sagged. "Uh, that was long time ago. Not recently."

"I see. Shell, the housekeeper, she said you were clearing the shower drains in the master bedroom a week before Mrs. Boggs was murdered."

"I had nothing to do with that."

"I didn't say you did. Were you in the master bathroom recently?"

"I forgot. Mr. Pena told me to clear the drains, that Mrs. Boggs was complaining it wasn't going down fast."

"Where else were you in the master suite?"

Sanchez's voice squeaked. "No place else."

"Were you in Mrs. Boggs' closet?"

"No, no. I wasn't."

I opened my folder and slid a picture to Sanchez. "What were you doing at Capital Pawn?"

He picked it up with his left hand. "Oh, yeah, my sister,

she found a ring and wanted to sell it."

"And where did she find this ring?"

"I think she said on the bus."

"You sure about that?"

"I don't really remember."

"The ring you tried to fence belonged to Mrs. Boggs."

"That's crazy, man. How can that be?"

"How? Simple, you stole it after you killed her."

"Hey, man, don't try to pin the murder on me."

"You took the ring but didn't kill her?"

"No, I didn't do it."

"Come on, Raul. It's a lot easier if you tell the truth about all this. We got you. We have you on camera."

"Okay, okay, I took the ring."

"Now we're getting somewhere. Where did you take the ring from?"

"Her closet."

"Is that where the necklace and other rings were?"

Sanchez's shoulder sagged.

"We know about the other jewelry, Raul. Were the other rings and necklace in the closet?"

He nodded.

"Where in the closet were they?"

"They were lying on top of a shelf. There was a whole mess of jewelry there. I didn't think she'd miss them."

"Did Mrs. Boggs catch you stealing them?"

"No."

"So, you killed her before robbing her jewelry?"

"I didn't touch her. I would never do something like that."

"You know what I think, Raul? I think you saw the jewelry when you were cleaning the drains. Then you thought it would be easy and you came back to steal a few pieces, but Mrs. Boggs confronted you and you panicked."

"No, no, that's not true and you know it."

"What I know is you're gonna be spending some time in jail until we figure all this out."

THE TRAFFIC on Bonita Beach Road was heavy and I was late again. About a hundred yards from Livingston Road, a text chimed its arrival. I was dying to see who it was from, but I didn't want to die in an accident either. I made a right and made my way to the Vasari turning lane where I took a peek; it was from Kayla.

I crossed over into Vasari's entrance and pulled over. It was encouraging to see the text was longer to read than the preview window allowed.

Taking a breath, I read it. Then read it again. Kayla apologized for not responding, saying she had been busy working and taking care of her mother. Then she said she hoped I was feeling well and to take care of myself. What did that mean?

31

LUCA

ON THE WAY TO OUR OFFICE AFTER LUNCH, WE WERE intercepted by a uniformed officer who said the sheriff wanted to see us. The new sheriff was becoming a sprained ankle. Thank goodness, he was only a placeholder. We took the stairs to the second floor and were quickly waved in to see the boss.

Frank Morgan looked up at Vargas and me but went back to thumbing through a file. A minute went by before he spoke.

"You went to see Gerey without asking first?"

"I don't understand, is there a problem, sir?"

"You should know better, Luca."

"We were following standard procedures."

"Standard? You see, Luca, that's where your Yankee roots went wrong."

"I'm sorry, sir, but I don't understand. It was just a routine visit."

"Routine? There's nothing routine about the Boggs. You understand?"

Vargas said, "Yes, sir. We realize how delicate the case is."

Morgan ran a hand over his flattop. "I want this case solved, but I want it done quietly. Last thing I need is a bunch of damn reporters out of Fort Myers crawling all over here."

Vargas said, "We'll do our best, Sheriff."

Morgan leaned forward. "Gerey gave me the rundown on the trust. There's a bunch of money at stake, ain't there?"

"All that money makes for plenty of motivation, if you ask me."

"I ain't asking. Just what do you think, I can't see a simple fact?"

Before I could respond, Vargas said, "It would be helpful if you could speak with the DA about getting the subpoena we requested."

Morgan eased back in his chair and smiled. "Already did. Now, you run off to them lawyers down the hall and see if they've got a judge to sign off on it yet."

In stereo, we said, "Yes, sir."

We fist-bumped as soon as we left Morgan's office, and headed to the prosecutor's office. The subpoena wasn't back yet, so we went down to our office to kill time before heading out to the Naples City Dock.

Sipping a coffee, I opened my emails and scrolled through them. One sender jumped off the screen. I hit enter.

"Hey, Vargas, guess what arrived?"

"My Christmas presents?"

"The Mexican police report on our boy Raul."

Vargas came around my desk and looked at a series of mug shots.

"That's him, all right. Look at the mug shot from his first arrest. He was just twenty-two, and from there you can see his descent into criminality in pictures."

"It's like he picked up a tattoo for every arrest."

"And looks like he was using drugs more and more."

"You know what? Today he looks more like he did as a twenty-year-old."

"Maybe he's cleaned himself up."

Vargas pointed and read over my shoulder. "He was also known as Raul Sandez."

"And a member of the Latin Kings gang. Those scumbags are into everything."

"Surprised it took him two years to steal anything."

"We don't know if that's true or not. Maybe nobody noticed."

"I don't know, Frank, you're the one who says greed gets small thieves to turn into bigger ones and then into inmates."

"That was pretty clever of me, don't you think?"

Vargas hit me on the top of my head. "I think we go see Sanchez or Sandez, but after we execute the search warrant on Gideon Brighthouse."

32

GIDEON BRIGHTHOUSE

THE SOUND OF A BOAT APPROACHING WOKE ME UP. I PICKED up the new biography on da Vinci off the floor and checked my watch. It was twenty after five. I slid a door to the deck open and went to the edge of the patio where the dock came into view.

What? A police boat was tying up and three people had disembarked. What did they want? I can't deal with all this. I darted back inside. Maybe I should make like I'm not here, or that I'm not feeling well. I needed a Valium, now.

As I put the bottle back in the medicine cabinet I heard a rapping on the glass door and a voice call out, "Mr. Brighthouse? It's the police."

Spinning my head around, I saw the master closet. It was a good place to hide, and I stepped toward it when I heard the housekeeper say that I was home. I took a couple of deep breaths and jumped into the bathroom, splashing water on my face.

The housekeeper was calling my name as she mounted the stairs. Dabbing my face with a hand towel, I stepped into the master hallway and told her I'd be right down. Looking in the mirror, I took five slow, deep breaths.

I paused at the top of the stairs. The detective guy who looked like George Clooney was holding my laptop, and his partner was rummaging through a drawer in my desk.

"Excuse me, please leave my things alone."

"Sorry, Mr. Brighthouse, we've got a court order."

"I . . . I don't understand. Who . . . who said you can do this?"

The woman detective held up a document and replied, "Judge Wilson."

Digging into my back pocket I pulled out my cell phone.

Detective Luca said, "What are doing?"

"Calling my lawyer."

"Not with that." He reached for my phone, and I took off for the deck. A uniformed officer stepped in front of me, snatching the phone out of my hand.

The female detective took out a pair of handcuffs as she walked over. "Mr. Brighthouse, we need you to calm down and cooperate or we'll have to restrain you."

I reached for a chair as light-headedness washed over me.

"I . . . I need my phone."

"You can use the house line, but you'll have to wait until we're finished here."

My knees wobbled, and she said, "Please, take a seat and try to remain calm. I know this is difficult for you, but there's no alternative."

Grabbing my chest, I said, "I . . . I need my Valium. I'm getting an attack. My chest is killing me. Hurry, it's in my medicine cabinet."

She called out to her partner to get the meds.

Breathing choppily, I said, "You have to . . . leave. Take

what you want. Just get out and . . . leave . . . leave me alone."

THE VALIUM finally wore off and I woke up on the couch. It was ten fifteen. Shell, the housekeeper, was watching TV in the den and noticed me as I made my way to the bathroom.

"Are you all right, Mr. Brighthouse?"

"Yeah, I'm okay."

"You sure, sir?"

"I'm fine. Were the police here earlier?"

She nodded. "You don't remember? You've got to be careful with them pills of yours."

I forced a smile. "I was hoping it was a bad dream."

"There are turkey sandwiches and fruit on the kitchen table. Why don't you have something to eat?"

"Thanks, Shell."

"Good night, sir."

Before she was off the deck, I'd already eaten half a sandwich. I was feeling better. Grabbing the other half, I went to see what the police had taken besides my cell and laptop.

No! No! I gasped and popped off my pillow. What's going on? It was just a dream, thank God. It felt so real. I thought I was actually stabbing Marilyn. I could recall the resistance as I plunged the knife in. I rubbed my face.

The clock said it was 2:35 a.m. I lay back down. Damn, that was frightening. I closed my eyes, but when I did, the image of Marilyn lying on the floor appeared.

I got out of bed and did my breathing to try and relax, but

my heart was still beating too fast. I sat in a chair and focused on my breath, feeling the air expand my chest before releasing it. After two cycles I was back to the image. I brought myself back to my breathing, but after another cycle a dead Marilyn flooded my head again.

Vaulting out of the chair, I headed to the bathroom and downed two Valiums. I paced the room for ten minutes until they started to kick in.

33

LUCA

Joan Hathaway met me at the door of her Port Royal home on Gin Lane. It looked about half the size of most surrounding homes. Still, it was worth around five million. I liked Hathaway right away. I was sure she had some facial work done, but she didn't have that plastic look.

From her front door you could see clear out the back of the house to the bay. "Beautiful home you have, ma'am."

"Thank you, we've been here for ages."

"What's the name of that bay out back?"

"Smuggler's Bay."

The view was magnificent. "I can see why you've stayed here so long."

She showed me into the formal living room, which threw me off. Though three crucifixes and two ancient looking icons hung on the walls, there were at least six Buddha statues and an object that looked like a steering wheel from an old ship.

"I just made lemonade. Let me get it. Sit anywhere."

When she left I took a close look at the wheel, trying to figure out what it was. Maybe this was from an ancient ship one of their ancestors piloted. Joan came in carrying a tray with a pitcher and glasses.

"I hope you don't mind me asking, but what is the significance of the wheel? Did it come off an old ship?"

She laughed. "My husband's a Buddhist, and as you can see, he collects artifacts. The wheel is called a Dharmachakra, and its eight spokes represent the eight noble paths central to Buddhism."

"Oh, I didn't know that."

"Neither did I until he brought it home. I'm a Catholic, and the only way to get him to stop bringing more Buddhas in was by putting up a crucifix up every time he did." She laughed and poured two glasses, handing one to me.

"Thanks. Since talking religion is taboo these days, let's get to Marilyn Boggs. We're trying to learn as much about her as possible. How long have you been friends?"

"I'm afraid to admit, will ages suffice?"

I smiled.

"Detective, you look like George Clooney, especially when you smile."

"I get that a lot. So, you've been friends for, what, twenty years?"

"At least. We met in high school but lost touch when she went to a finishing school. Boy, that sounds like it's from a different era, doesn't it? Marilyn and I reconnected when she came back and landed at the United Way when I was president of the Collier chapter."

"Did she tell you about her marital difficulties?"

She frowned. "I'm not comfortable talking about such private matters."

I leaned forward. "Please, Joan, we need to understand what was going on in her life if we are to nail the SOB that did this."

"I understand. Marilyn seemed happy with Gideon for a couple of years. Then she started making comments. This was after he had a heart attack. She said that he was a basket case and was losing his mind. I felt bad for Gideon and reminded her of the old saying." Using her fingers to make air quotes, she continued, " 'In sickness and in health,' but when I did, she said life was too short."

"Did she tell you about her extramarital affairs?"

She nodded. "She didn't say much until she started seeing John Barnet. Then she was like a teenager, trying to tell me things I frankly had no interest in hearing. I've been married to the same man for thirty years and couldn't imagine doing what she did, especially with him."

"You knew Barnet?"

"Unfortunately."

"Why is that?"

"He's not trustworthy, and that is more than just my opinion."

"Can you elaborate? It might be important."

"Well, on at least three occasions he overcharged us. It was like he was testing us, and when it slipped by, he upped the ante. The one that stuck out was for thirty thousand dollars. That's a lot of money, and we're a charitable organization with limited resources."

"What did he say about the overcharges?"

"When I challenged the excessive charge, he said it was a mistake, that he had a new girl handling the invoicing and that she had confused the billing on two events." She took a sip of lemonade. "Mistakes happen, but I've seen quite a few gals in this town get taken in by . . . by his type. So, I audited all of Barnet's invoices, and what do you know, I found two more. What really got to me was the fact he was testing us. The first one was just over a thousand, and when it slipped through, he bumped the next one to fifteen thousand."

"How did Mrs. Boggs react when all this happened?"

Hathaway pulled her lips in. "She defended him, said it was an honest mistake. I was stunned. I warned her that he was not to be trusted."

"Did he make good for the overcharges?"

She nodded.

I pulled out my notebook. "I have a few names of her friends: Susan Malloy, Jessica Cloydon, Betty Sue Grapple, and Maria Corsica. Is there anyone else you think we should check with?"

"Marilyn had a wide circle of friends. You've got the one's she was friends with for a long time. You might want to talk with Patty Clermont. After Patty got divorced the two of them got close."

I jotted the name down. "Is she local?"

Joan nodded. "After her divorce, Patty moved to the Moorings. Let me get my phone. I've got her number."

34

LUCA

WHEN SHE OPENED THE DOOR, I HESITATED BEFORE SPEAKING. Patty Clermont didn't look like the image I'd formed. As a friend of Marilyn's, I'd expected someone older, who resembled Joan Hathaway. Patty Clermont, bouncing on the balls of her feet and ponytail swinging, exuded an electricity you didn't expect in the Moorings.

"Patty Clermont?"

"That's me," she smiled.

"I'm Detective Luca, with the sheriff's office. We've been checking with people who knew Marilyn Boggs. We were given your name by a longtime friend of hers."

She swung the door wide open, the breeze blousing the white gauze dress she wore.

"Come on in."

The home had a wide-open floor plan that contrasted with its more traditional front. I wondered when she'd renovated the home. As we got deeper into the home, the music that was playing got louder. A quartet of sliders opened the house to a small yard, dominated by a glass-tiled pool. A wall of vegetation provided privacy from neighbors that were just a few feet away. If this place had a view, it would go for three million, provided the front was redone.

She kicked her flip-flops off and sat on a gray leather sofa, tucking her legs under and to the side.

"Make yourself comfy."

I sat in a low-backed, red chair made of corduroy and said, "How long have you known Marilyn?"

She eyed me and wet her lips before saying, "We knew each other a long time but didn't really socialize much until we worked on the Juvenile Diabetes Ball. We had a lot of fun putting the event together, and it carried over. We kinda lost touch a bit. Then, when I was going through a difficult time with my divorce and all, Marilyn was there for me. She was really great, got me out of the house. She knew everyone."

"What did you know about her relationship with her husband?"

"Things weren't good."

She stood up, sucked in her tummy and smoothed the front of her dress.

"I need a cocktail. Can I get one for you?"

"Sorry, but I'm on the job."

"You've got to learn to loosen up, Detective. By the way, you look very familiar."

As she poured herself a vodka, I asked, "You said things weren't good. What do you mean by that?"

She brushed against my knees on her way back to the sofa. "They'd drifted apart. It started when Gideon began having issues."

"Did she tell you what those issues were?"

"It was anxiety, you know, panic attacks. And he never wanted to leave the house. It was almost like he was a hermit. It's crazy, when you think he used to be in politics."

"Did you know about her extramarital activities?"

She threw her head back, laughing. "That's a lot of words to say she was having affairs. Yeah, she told me about them."

"What did she tell you?"

"She was having a good time, especially with the guy, John, who owns that wine store in Waterside. He was a smoothie, made her feel good."

"And all she said about him and the relationship was that she was having a good time?"

She smiled slyly. "Don't tell me you want the saucy parts, Detective."

"We're all adults here, Ms. Clermont. Anything you tell me is held in strict confidence and would be used for the investigation only."

She studied me for a moment. "I'm not really sure I understand what you mean."

"Anything that was unusual, it doesn't have to be sexual, just anything, even the smallest thing you think might be helpful in drawing a complete picture of her and John Barnet."

She giggled. "You mean like if they were doing any S and M type thing?"

"That could be something."

"Well, no way Marilyn would never, at least she didn't tell me about it, do something like that. I mean, she got twisted when he filmed them together."

I leaned forward. "When they were having sex?"

"That seems to have got your attention. Does pornography turn you on, Detective?"

Heat flashed up my cheeks. "Not at all. It's an interesting detail. You said she was twisted over it."

"You look even cuter when you blush."

"Marilyn was mad about the filming, right?"

After a quick pout, she nodded. "She was upset about it because he did it without her permission."

"Why? She would have let him do it as long as she knew?"

She put her feet on the cocktail table, revealing some of her fine china. "No, no. She didn't like the idea at all. He told her he did it to add a little spice. You ask me, I think she was upset because it kinda suggests he was growing tired of her."

She was gunning for me, but even if I could cross the line, and my dad told me never to shit in your own backyard, I'd never run with someone like her. Looking over her head into the yard, I asked, "You seem to be saying the relationship was drawing to a close. Is that something she told you?"

"Not directly, but us girls, we know when things ain't right."

So, this was where the term, "pulling teeth" came from. "Do you have something more than a feeling?"

She smiled and writhed like a snake. "Feeling it is what it's all about. Don't you agree?"

I was getting ready to strangle her. "I need to understand what makes you believe they were having troubles."

"About a month ago Marilyn got really quiet, and that's not like her. I asked her what was wrong, and she said nothing. But I knew it had to be him, so I said, "It's John, isn't it?" Marilyn nodded yes, but when I asked her if she wanted to talk about it, she said no."

"Anything else?"

"Well, Marilyn wasn't herself ever again. She seemed distracted. I tried to talk to her, but she said she didn't want to talk about it."

35

LUCA

Sheriff Morgan was pulling on a cowboy boot when Vargas and I were shown into his office, and he said, "Pardon me, ma'am, but it felt like I had a piece of glass in my foot, but there's nothing there."

I said, "You might want to check with a doctor. It sounds like you may have a plantar wart."

"Plantar wart? Is that something you Yanks brought down here too?"

Vargas said, "It's actually pretty common down here, Sheriff. Might be because we wear a lot of flip-flops and sandals."

Raising his boot up, he said, "Well, how the heck did I get something like that? I just about wear these to bed."

We all had a quick laugh before Morgan said, "We've got to tread carefully here with Mr. Brighthouse, or Gerey will have the dogs nipping at me."

"We understand, sir. Detective Luca and I have discussed our interview strategy, but we're open to hearing your ideas on it."

"Heck, you're the detectives on this case, and besides,

Luca's got big-city experience." Morgan put his elbows on the desk and looked at each of us before saying, "I just want to make sure we measure at least twice before cutting."

Vargas and I bobbed our heads and Morgan said, "I don't want this case hanging open when the new sheriff takes over, so go do what you know how to do."

GIDEON BRIGHTHOUSE and Peter Gerey were waiting in a black Ford Explorer parked in the rear lot. An officer was sent to tell them we were ready. It was the first time in ages that I hadn't been able to keep someone stewing before interviewing them. The disruption in routine watered the seeds of self-doubt rattling around in my head.

As agreed, I went to meet them at the rear entrance. There was a bear of a man walking with Gerey and Brighthouse. What was he doing here? Was he with Gerey? It was Bill Crowley, a high-profile criminal attorney. The doubt seeds sprouted. I wondered if Morgan had tipped off Gerey on what we had found.

Crowley's hand swallowed mine when we shook. While we headed to the interview room, everyone but Gideon made small talk. We got to the door, and as Crowley and Vargas entered, I pulled Gerey aside and said, "What's up with Crowley?"

"You know criminal law is not my area of expertise, Detective."

"Why does Brighthouse need a criminal lawyer all of a sudden?"

"We'd like to avoid the possibility of a misunderstanding."

"So, you hire a top gun like him?"

"The family has had Crowley on retainer for a decade."

"Really? And what about the family keeping a low profile?"

"I can assure you, there won't be any leaking coming from our team. And Detective, I hope I don't need to remind you that my client is under the care of several doctors, both medical and psychiatric. As you ask your questions, I hope you'll keep in mind that his emotional state is tenuous."

"As long as he cooperates, we're fine."

"Good. Shall we get this started?"

A fidgety Brighthouse brushed the seat of the plastic chair with his hand before sandwiching himself between his lawyers. He was wearing a pair of light yellow slacks and a blue linen shirt, providing a slice of color to the drab room.

Nodding at Vargas, I hit the record button and she stated the attendees, location, date, and time. Formalities covered, I began.

"Mr. Brighthouse, pursuant to a search warrant, we confiscated a mobile phone and laptop that belonged to you, as well as an iPad and phone belonging to your wife, Marilyn Boggs. You were present during the search, and we left an inventory receipt for the items, correct?"

Brighthouse eyes were dull and he didn't respond. Crowley gave him an elbow and whispered in his ear.

"Ah, yes . . . it was very . . . upsetting."

"Are these the only electronics you own?"

He blinked a couple of times. "Yes."

"Nothing like an iPod or Kindle reader?"

"I prefer . . . to hold and read . . . a physical book. It's more personal."

"Did you lend your electronics to anyone, Mr. Brighthouse?"

"No."

Brighthouse took a sip of water.

"So, no one else used or had access to your laptop or phone?"

"As far . . . as I'm aware."

Gerey glanced at Crowley, who said, "There are a number of people who work on the island, in addition to the deceased, who had access to Mr. Brighthouse's electronics, among his other possessions."

Vargas said, "Noted, though the remoteness of Keewaydin Island dramatically reduces the number of people with possible access."

Crowley said, "Reduce, maybe, but not eliminate the possibility."

I said, "Is there any particular reason you searched the Internet for poison, Mr. Brighthouse?"

Brighthouse stiffened and reached for his water. "Poison? I don't . . . recall."

"Let us freshen your memory then. Detective Vargas, can you help him remember?"

Vargas opened the file in front of her. "This is a list compiled by the electronics division in the Collier County Crime Lab." She held up three pages. "It documents the browsing activity on the laptop confiscated during the search on Keewaydin Island."

I said, "There are over eighty searches for poisons and a dozen on electrical fires. It seems Mr. Brighthouse was trying to decide on just how to kill his wife."

Brighthouse began to squirm. Crowley put a hand on his forearm and said, "Searching the Internet isn't a crime."

I grabbed the file and held up a document. "Not in itself, but he also browsed sites that detailed how much it would take to kill a human. And this history proves he researched and sought fatal poisons in more than enough quantity to kill his wife."

Crowley took a brief look at the receipt and said, "It makes for a nice story, but Marilyn Boggs died of stab wounds."

I tossed the papers toward them. "It shows a premeditated intent to kill."

Crowley said, "If you're planning to charge my client for the death of his wife, I'd like to remind you that planning a murder and failing to act on it is not a crime."

"Noted, Counselor, but wouldn't you say, since we have Marilyn Boggs' dead body, that his plan was put into action?"

"If you have evidence connecting Gideon Brighthouse with the stabbing death of his beloved wife, Marilyn, I suggest you reveal it. Otherwise, I believe it's time for us to go."

I said, "I'm sure you'd like to know that in addition to finding a way to burn his wife to death, your client researched various poisons, even from a blowfish, going so far as to check on Japanese restaurants to stage the crime. I'd say that certainly qualifies as proof he was looking for a way to kill his wife without implicating himself."

"You weave a nice tale, Detective. But without evidence, there's nothing to implicate my client, just a nice little story."

Crowley stood and Gerey popped to his feet so fast he stirred Brighthouse from his listlessness. Last time he was here he bolted; this time he looked ready for a nap. Crowley grabbed Brighthouse by the elbow and lifted him out of the chair.

36

GIDEON BRIGHTHOUSE

CROWLEY WAS A BIG MAN WITH ROUGH HANDS. I DIDN'T LIKE it when he patted me on the back or grabbed my arm to tell me something. He was so different from Peter Gerey, it was tough to believe they were both lawyers. I didn't want a criminal lawyer. It made me look like I had something to hide. I told Gerey how I felt, but he said to protect me from unfair prosecution we needed a lawyer with his experience. And that's how I ended up with Crowley.

It was no longer a feeling; this was real. I was losing control of my life. Everyone told me not to take any additional meds, but I had no choice. I couldn't risk another meltdown at the police station, so ten minutes before we left Keewaydin I started nursing a water bottle with two crushed Valiums in it.

It was tough to concentrate. I tried to remember what my lawyers told me yesterday. It wasn't easy opening up, especially with Gerey. His allegiance was definitely with the family, so I was on guard to see if they were going to gang up on me. Still, I had to be honest and admit that our marriage was terrible and that I had fantasized about her being dead. I qualified it, stressing that I could never do it.

I think they actually believed me. When they asked me about what could be on my laptop I told them I'd looked up poisons, but that was during times when I was depressed and thought of doing myself in. They said nothing, but I knew they didn't buy it. The good thing was when Crowley said it wasn't a crime to plan to kill someone. He said that unless there was some proof connecting me directly to the stabbing, we had nothing to worry about.

That's what I thought about as I walked into the interview room. It was stark white, like an empty canvas. I wondered what Keith Haring would do to a room like this. It'd be something to see. That would make some exhibit—a room painted by Haring would immerse you in creativity. Crowley nudged me toward a dusty chair.

After brushing it off, I sat and realized the interview had started. Focusing was hard, and my mind drifted to when Crowley asked me if I had any child pornography on my laptop or phone. Did he think I was a twisted pervert? Crowley gave me an elbow and repeated the detective's question.

Like I could forget about the search? My head was heavy. I pinched my thigh and scratched at a node on my linen pants. I took another gulp. How long was this going to last?

The detective wanted to know about my laptop. I answered, but then Crowley went back at them. He was sounding pretty good to me, but then they started asking about the poisons I'd been researching. This was bad. I didn't know what to say. Then Crowley patted my arm and told the police it wasn't criminal to search the web.

Detective Luca was getting angry, and he and Crowley went back and forth. What a relief. It was like I wasn't there.

Crowley was so fast, I had trouble keeping up with what he was saying. He was amazing and had things under control. I took another sip when I heard him say it was time to go.

Was that going to be it? Much as I wanted this over, I was dead tired and needed to rest. A tight clasping on my elbow aroused me, and suddenly I was on my feet heading for the door. I couldn't believe it; we were done.

I climbed into the SUV and watched my lawyers talk through the window. They shook hands. Crowley walked away, while Gerey got into the seat next to me.

I said, "Thank you for getting him. He was magnificent today."

Putting his seat belt on, Gerey said, "We're a long way from this being over, Gideon."

What did he mean a long way?

Then Gerey looked me in the eye and said, "I realize these situations are stressful for you, Gideon. However, you're not going to help yourself by being overmedicated."

37

LUCA

ON MY WAY TO INTERROGATE RAUL SANCHEZ, AKA SANDEZ, I was beginning to feel like I'd never buy a home in Naples. Another bid, this time on a two-bedroom in Kensington, was rejected as too low again. The sellers didn't even counter, which I didn't get. Instead of getting emotional about it, they should just counter. The Kensington location was great, but the place needed a complete renovation. I didn't have the stomach and probably the cash for a total gut job.

How could sellers not see how much updating their twenty-five-year-old place needed? Probably because in other parts of the country the updating cycle was decades longer. People in New York will tolerate forty-year-old kitchens and bathrooms, but not down here. I had only a couple of months to find a house and close on it. Otherwise I'd have to find another place to rent, since my landlord's sister was taking over my coach home.

Vargas said that if I got into a jam I could stay in the cabana suite she had. With a separate entrance and its own bathroom, it was a perfect setup for short-term stays. But it'd be weird staying on her property, and though I didn't cook much, it only had a sink and small fridge.

My cell buzzed. Man, Vargas had a sixth sense.

"Where are you, Frank?"

"On my way, Mom."

"You're late."

"I took a ride up to Bonita to see a couple of places."

"Anything interesting?"

"I didn't get inside. Just wanted to see the communities and how far. That's why I'm running behind. And the bad news is that they're too far north to do each day. I'm starting to feel the pressure."

"The offer on the cabana is always there. It's no big deal."

"Thanks. I appreciate it, but I'd like to save myself another move, if you know what I mean?"

"Trust me, I get it."

"How's our jewel thief?"

"It's not him we got to worry about. His lawyer is getting restless, threatening to cancel the interview, said he has to be in court soon."

"I'm ten minutes away. Offer them something to drink. If they get crazy, start without me."

My pee alarm went off as I jogged down the hall to inter-rogation room three. Could I risk sitting on the toilet trying to coax number one out? It always took at least ten to fifteen minutes, time I didn't have.

I looked at the camera feed; Vargas was talking. I tucked my shirt and my urge in and entered. Raul Sanchez was mid-sentence.

"They made a mistake, that's all. My mother's maiden name is Sanchez. My father, who I never met, had a last name like hers, Sandez. Check the birth records, you'll see."

Vargas said, "Detective Luca has joined the interview."

I nodded at Raul and Joe Girona, a new kid from the public defender's office. Vargas said, "You continued to use both names while in Mexico?"

"Look, I was a kid and I didn't know what to do."

His attorney said, "Mexican law requires the use of both your mother's maiden name and the father's last name. Raul's official name in Mexico is Raul Sanchez Sandez."

Two last names? How could that be? I looked at Vargas. She responded, "I'm fully aware that due to the vast numbers of Hispanics with surnames such as Perez, Martinez, and the like, that Mexico requires both parents last names to separate identities."

Really? How come I never knew that?

Vargas continued, "Perhaps your client can tell us why he had two Mexican driver licenses? One issued to Raul Sandez Sanchez, and the other to Raul Sanchez Sandez."

Raul spoke, "In Mexico, the fines get higher for each ticket. So, to avoid paying too much, I had two licenses."

"I see, it was all about parking tickets, then. Nothing to do about all the arrests you were piling up?"

"My client has already responded to your question."

I said, "You were a member of the Latin Kings gang. That's a rough crew."

"Is there a question in there, Detective?"

I said, "You want to come clean? What happened at the Boggs home on Keewaydin?"

"I told you, man. I was cleaning the shower drain and I saw all this jewelry. I know I shouldn't have taken it, but I was behind on my rent. You see, my mom got sick and I needed money."

Once again, the old 'my mom was sick' excuse was rolled out. I said, "You know, Raul, your credibility would be a lot higher if you didn't have this?" I picked up his Mexican rap sheet.

"That was then. I don't do that stuff anymore. That's why I left Mexico, to start fresh, stay clean."

"But you fell back into your old criminal ways, didn't you?"

"My mother—"

"I realize it's no excuse, but his mother is, in fact, battling kidney cancer."

"You're right, Counselor, it's no excuse for killing Marilyn Boggs."

"I didn't kill no one."

Vargas said, "Your rap sheet says that you were arrested for suspicion of murder."

Sanchez shook his head. "But that was almost ten years ago."

I said, "It establishes a pattern. Once you kill the first time, there's no telling where it ends."

"My client has admitted to taking the jewelry. What we have here are charges of robbery, nothing more."

"Your client made his so-called admission after being caught lying. How can anyone trust what he says? You want to know what I think? I think Raul Sanchez Sandez realized how trusting the Boggs were, and when they gave him a job that had him in the privacy of the bedroom, he violated the trust he was given. He rummaged through their belongings and concocted a plan to return to steal her jewelry, and when he did, Marilyn Boggs confronted him and he stabbed her to death."

The attorney checked his watch. "My client denies any involvement in the death of Marilyn Boggs."

I said, "Raul, as Detective Vargas stated, you were arrested and are being held on suspicion of murder. I find it interesting that according to the Mexican Federal Police, the victim was killed with a knife."

"I got nothing to say. Those charges were dropped."

"Dropped? Not quite. You plead guilty to harboring a fugitive, a punk from your gang."

"I don't see the relevancy of an old case Mexican case."

"Really, Counselor? Your client was charged in a murder down in Mexico, and the woman whose jewelry he admits to stealing is dead. Both were stabbed to death. That's damn relevant to me."

"It appears to me that you're fishing, Detective. If you have anything that proves your allegations, let's hear it." He stood. "I've got to be in court in twenty minutes."

This young lawyer was tough. I hoped he'd leave the public defender's office to earn real money, otherwise I could see him haunting me until I retired.

38

LUCA

"Mr. Pena, thank you for coming in to talk with us."

"Whatever I can do to help catch the person who did this to Mrs. Boggs, I'll do."

I checked my notes, and his leathery face fit the sixty-two it said he was. Eduardo Pena was sturdily built, not particularly muscular, but rock-solid and not much older looking than forty-five.

"You've worked for the Boggs a long time."

"Yes, almost twenty years now."

He never looked me in the eyes for more than a second or two. Normally, that'd make me suspicious, but with Pena I knew it was a way for him to be deferential.

"You hired Raul Sanchez?"

He frowned. "Yes, but he was recommended by Frank Perez, a contractor I've known for a long time. Perez feels almost as bad as I do about all of this."

"Don't beat yourself up, Eduardo, Sanchez didn't have a record, in the States anyway."

"You mean he had a record in Mexico?"

"I'm afraid so."

"But he said he came here about ten years ago."

"Eight, actually, and either he kept his nose clean or just never got caught."

Pena wagged his head. "He fooled me. I should have known better."

"Sanchez didn't give you any reason to be concerned? No hints he was up to no good?"

"No, he did his job and kept quiet. I'm pretty sure even Mrs. Boggs liked him. I saw her talking to him a couple of days before she, she was murdered."

"Really? Was that something he did regularly, talking to her?"

"No. I always tell my guys to stay out of the way, to be invisible."

"Any idea what they may have been talking about?"

He shook his head. "It could've been about anything."

I handed him my card. "Do me a favor and ask the rest of your crew if they knew why he was talking to Mrs. Boggs. If you find out anything, let me—"

"Sure, no problem."

"Did you know any of his friends? Did he bring anyone onto the island?"

"No. It's not permitted to have anyone not invited by the family on the island."

"Do you know anything about Sanchez's family?"

"Just that his mother was pretty sick. I think something with the kidneys."

"Can you think of anything unusual, out of the ordinary, no matter how small, involving Raul Sanchez?"

"I wish there was something, but I can't think of anything."

"If something comes to mind, anything, let me know."

"Okay. Say, you don't think he had anything to do with her murder, do you?"

"Sorry, Eduardo, but I can't comment on that."

VARGAS and I finished taking statements from the staff at Paradise Granite. A slab of gray stone had fallen onto a worker, nearly severing his lower leg. Though the driver of the forklift stated the piece had slipped off, two other laborers supported the injured man's claim that it was an intentional act.

Viewing the footage from a camera that was too far from the scene and in a warehouse that was poorly lit, didn't help us determine who was right. We took the video, confident the lab would be able to tell us whether we had an attempted murder on our hands, and left.

Driving along Shirley Street in our black Crown Victoria, the conversation quickly moved from the workplace incident to the Marilyn Boggs murder.

"What's your gut telling you, Vargas? I don't like this Sanchez guy one bit, but the husband clearly had motive and was planning to off her."

"If we hadn't uncovered the Mexican gang involvement, I'd say Sanchez was just a thief. Now, I'm not so sure."

"I know what you mean."

Stopped for a red light at the corner of Pine Ridge, Vargas said, "Like you say, though, most murders are committed by someone close to the victim. The marriage was in shambles, and the husband, no matter what he says, was humiliated, made to look like a fool."

"He confronted them the day she was killed."

"And he looked for ways to kill her."

I said, "And the good old trust was packed with twenty-million reasons to do it."

"We need something that ties him to the stabbing. A break of some kind."

"How many times have we said that in the last couple of years? Every case hits a wall. I don't care which one, they all do. We do what we always do, stay on it and we'll make our own break."

"Is that false bravado I hear?"

She was right, but sometimes you got to fake it to make it. "No, I really believe it."

We drove silently for five minutes when I said, "Getting back to Sanchez, one thing that bothers me is why didn't he steal a whole bunch of jewelry, not to mention, what, fifty K sitting in the bedroom?"

"Maybe he was trying to keep his job, just take a few items, not turn it into a blowout."

"If that was the case, it wouldn't have lasted. His greed would've pushed him to up the stakes."

"I don't know, Frank. Maybe he was doing a lot of low-key crimes the whole time he's been in the States."

"Well, he'd be the first guy to keep his greed under control so he wouldn't get busted."

"But he didn't, he got caught."

"Something has been bothering me. The fifty thousand in cash. I know these people are in a different league, but I read somewhere Warren Buffet doesn't even carry a wallet around with him. Why would anybody in today's world of ATMs, PayPal, and wire transfers need that much cash?"

"Maybe as a hedge against a catastrophe?"

"I don't buy it. They wouldn't be alone in a disaster; the family office probably has several well-stocked bunkers laid out in the event of a disaster."

"You can't say they're not thorough."

I pulled into a turning lane and she said, "What are you doing?"

"I just thought of something. We need to talk with Sanchez."

"You going to clue me in, Frank?"

39

LUCA

STARING AT THE WHITEBOARD WE KEPT WITH ALL THE players of the case, I kept coming back to the affair. Octopus-like, it had several tentacles that could have led to murder. Did Gideon kill her out of jealousy, or to make sure he'd get twenty million from the trust? Did Marilyn want a divorce but didn't want to take the hit the trust would take, leading her to try to kill Gideon and he retaliated? Was it a lover's quarrel with Barnet that got out of hand?

I read through my notes. Reviewing the Marilyn Boggs and John Barnet relationship raised a question about its trajectory. Patty Clermont thought it had slowed down and even said Marilyn had grown quiet about the affair.

Asking her some pointed questions would clear up the timeline, but I didn't want to get in front of her like I should. She wasn't my type, but I had learned not to risk it; there was only so much willpower left in this forty-two-year-old. Using the phone to do an interview wasn't only not protocol but left me without any body language to read. And her body was Pulitzer Prize-reading material.

I punched her number in before I changed my mind.

"Miss Clermont? It's Detective Luca."

"Oh, what a pleasant surprise. How's my Clooney clone?"

That was clever. I'd never heard it put that way. "I'd like to ask you a question."

"Yes, I'm free tomorrow night."

They call aggressive woman cougars, but this Clermont was in a league of her own.

"I wanted to ask about Marilyn and John Barnet. When we met, you said you thought the relationship was cooling off. Do you remember?"

"I never forget a handsome man, especially when he shows up at my door."

It was uncomfortable but mildly reassuring that I had pinned her within minutes of meeting her.

"It's important that I understand the timeline, the arc of their relationship. Can you do that for me?"

"Anything, Detective, believe me, anything you want."

The sound of a leaf blower came through the phone. "Good. You said that Marilyn was like a schoolgirl when she started the affair with Barnet. Is that accurate?"

"Marilyn was head over heels. It was refreshing to see someone unabashedly enjoying herself."

"Did she ever mention getting divorced from her husband?"

"Not really. It wasn't about Gideon. You men never seem to understand; it was about her."

Was Clermont another woman whose divorce transformed them into a feminist? "Can you clear up 'not really'? Did she discuss it or not?"

"I took any talk of divorce, which was kinda general, as Marilyn venting. Not a plan, just like a release for her."

"I get it. Would you find it surprising that Gideon claims she had told him she wanted a divorce?"

"I like to think the two of us were close, so I can't really imagine her not telling me about something like that. But, in reality, nothing would surprise me, Detective, unless you came over."

"You mentioned the episode where Barnet allegedly filmed them having sex."

"It wasn't allegedly, he did it."

"Previously, you said you thought it was to spice up their sex life. You thought Barnet was getting bored."

"It could have been. Marilyn, after she got over being filmed, was concerned about it."

"After the filming episode, did the relationship begin to fade?"

"Marilyn was angry about being filmed, and for about a week, things were in a funk. But Marilyn, she couldn't stay mad long. It was one of the things I loved and frankly admired about her. She was a special girl."

If you were as wealthy as the Boggs, I'm willing to bet you'd also have a hard time staying mad.

"The relationship got back on track?"

"Yeah. Things seemed to be going good for them again."

"How long did this good period last?"

"A week or two."

"Then you said something about her was different."

"She changed, got real quiet and wouldn't talk about Barnet. Something was bothering her, and it had to do with him. I'm sure about that."

40

GIDEON BRIGHTHOUSE

I TIPPED MY EMPTY BOTTLE OVER AND SHOOK THE LAST DROPS into my mouth as soon as Gerey got out of the SUV. Just what did he mean by 'long way to go'?

By the time we were back on 41, the mirage Crowley had created dissipated. I was in trouble. As soon as I got to the island I would have to destroy the mushrooms. Burning them would be the best way; nothing but ashes I could mix into the gulf. I'd have to be careful not to breathe any fumes in; it could fatal. What a twist that would make.

I'd have to get rid of them before the police found them. That couldn't happen. It would give them physical proof and I'd be doomed. I'd never survive living in a small cell; I'd die of a heart attack the first night. Dealing with the mushrooms was dangerous but they had to go.

When the driver repeated that he was driving as fast as he could, the idea to ask Gerey about how much trouble the mushrooms would be for me popped into my head. Maybe I didn't have to risk getting rid of them, but would Gerey give me up to the family? There was attorney-client privilege preventing him, but with his bread buttered by the Boggs, he'd find a way to tip them off.

What about Crowley? He was a criminal lawyer, defending all kinds of people, most of whom probably did what they were accused of. He was used to keeping information confidential. I could ask him. That's what I'd do.

Pulling up to the dock, I realized Crowley was brought in by Gerey and would have to report what I told him to Gerey. The thought of dealing with such a toxic substance brought a tightness between my shoulders that worsened as we climbed onto the yacht. Why hadn't I hidden a second bottle of Valium-laced water on board?

My heart started pounding as I remembered Gerey telling me to lay off my meds. How was I supposed to get through all this? I was sick. Everyone knew I couldn't handle this. How long till we get to Keewaydin? I hung my head over the side, but it was nowhere in sight.

As we rounded the corner off Galleon, I could see Nelsons Walk and the northeast tip of Keewaydin. It never looked so good.

41

LUCA

I READ THROUGH THE REPORT AND FELT WE HAD GOTTEN THE break we were looking for.

The geeks in the crime lab had identified a transaction that Brighthouse had made with a Russian entity called Beatrice Solutions. Russia? Again? When the firm didn't respond to the lab, they requested assistance from the Russian Politsiya. I was surprised the Russkies responded so quickly, confirming that Beatrice had sold and shipped a lethal quantity of death cap mushrooms to Brighthouse.

This was no longer wishful thinking by Brighthouse. He took action and purchased a deadly poison to kill his wife. Once we found the mushrooms, it'd provide us with physical evidence of his intent. It was something to work with, thanks to the geeks and the Russians, of all people.

Googling death cap mushrooms, I understood why Gideon chose them; they were the deadliest mushrooms and resembled edible types. The death cap grew wild throughout Europe, and its poisonous amatoxins could withstand cooking temperatures.

These mushrooms were nasty. A few hours after

consumption a person would experience violent abdominal pain, vomiting, and bloody diarrhea. Then the liver, kidneys, and central nervous system would begin shutting down, leading to coma and death. What a terrible way to go. Gideon must've really hated his wife.

I couldn't help thinking how the father had set all this in motion with his penalties on divorce. How would the old man feel if he knew this was the way his son-in-law planned to kill his little girl?

I was on the phone when Vargas breezed into the office. She was wearing corduroy pants that really highlighted her figure. She was about to pick up the phone, but I waved her off and finished my call.

Waving the report, I said, "Guess what the geeks in computer forensics hunted down?"

"Brighthouse?"

"Yup. Gideon, snake that he is, bought deadly mushrooms from some Russian website."

"He took action?"

"Big time. These mushrooms, they're called death caps, are fatal. You only need a minuscule amount, and they look like ordinary mushrooms."

"I'll bet he was gonna put some of it in with the other veggies she juiced."

I hated to admit it, but I'd forgotten about the juicer sitting on the counter.

"That's right. Poor woman would never know she'd be mixing her own death cocktail. There's been a bunch of people, even famous ones, like Pope Clement and a Roman Emperor, who ate them accidentally and bought the farm."

"Really?"

"It's a super nasty way to go. Makes me want to nail this guy even more."

"Is it an illegal substance?"

"No, it grows wild all over Europe. It's not altered, like ricin is."

"That's from the castor oil plant, right?"

"Yeah, the seeds of it. Man, I wish these mushrooms were illegal. If they were, we could haul Brighthouse in here and pressure his ass."

"Think we can concoct a plan to fool him that he's violated the law?"

"I like the idea, but I can't see it getting by Crowley and Gerey."

42

LUCA

Walking along the jumping water fountains, I turned the corner, passed the Louis Vuitton store, and there he was. Seated, arm across the back of a bench, was Barnet. A streak of yellow sock peeked out of the bottom of his white khakis, matching his shirt. Eyes closed, his face was tilted toward the sun. Was he looking to the sun to offset his shadiness?

I studied him for a moment before noticing the red sale banner visible beyond his shoulder. Fifty percent off wines? That was a significant markdown; maybe I could try one of those wines he was so fond of.

"Mr. Barnet?"

Arm sweeping off the back of the bench, he said, "What? Oh, uh, hello."

"Catching a few rays?"

"Taking a short break. You out shopping?"

"Not exactly. You have a couple of minutes?"

Barnet looked at his watch. "Um, I don't know. I've got an appointment."

"It'll be quick."

Barnet stood. "Can we talk as we walk? Nothing against the police, but it's not good for business."

"I understand."

We headed toward Saks, our eyes following the rears of two package-laden women.

"No shortage of women buying two-thousand-dollar pocketbooks."

"I'd love to convert them to collectors of Bordeaux."

"I see you're running a pretty big sale. Business not so good?"

"It's not too bad. We need to clean out some inventory."

"Did Marilyn carry a lot of cash with her?"

Barnet stutter-stepped. "Cash? No, I don't think so. But it's not like I went through her bag."

"You did a significant amount of business with her, didn't you?"

"I wouldn't characterize it as significant. But, yes, Barnet's handled quite a few functions for Marilyn."

"Didn't you do all of her functions?"

"I'd like to think. Barnet's always delivered for her, but you never know."

It always rubbed me the wrong way when people talked about themselves in the third person. What was up with that? Trying too hard to elevate themselves? I could play along, though.

"We've been told there a couple of times when Barnet's overcharged for its services."

"Much as we try, we're not above making a minor mistake."

"As I understand it, it was more significant than minor."

"I'd have to check into the particulars."

"Did Barnet's overcharge any client's other than Marilyn Boggs?"

Barnet stopped, looked both ways, and said, "Detective Luca, I resent the inference that my relationship with Marilyn had anything to do with anything but us making a simple mistake."

"As I understand it, it was more than one mistake. In fact, people who are familiar with the circumstance believe the overcharges were orchestrated knowingly by Barnet's."

"Really? If they have proof, then why not bring charges?"

"You know full well that charities would endanger themselves if they revealed they'd been taken. They'd lose the trust of their supporters."

"Detective, I have to stop you there. You're using words that are slanderous to Barnet's and I don't appreciate it."

It was false outrage but no sense having him get too defensive.

"Fair enough. Is there any reason that Marilyn would have fifty thousand in cash sitting in her nightstand?"

He paused, then stroked his Van Dyke. The question was whether it was feigned thoughtfulness or real.

"As you know, they're extremely wealthy. I can't see why she would, but I really don't know."

"Anything illicit, like drugs, that would have necessitated cash?"

He smiled. "No, not with Marilyn. Maybe she paid the staff in cash. Lord knows, there are enough of them."

"Did she tell you that some of her jewelry had been stolen?"

"Yes. She was heartbroken, especially about the ring her father had given her."

"Did she give you any reason to think she was being blackmailed?"

"Uh, blackmailed? No, why do you say that?"

"Just exploring possible motives."

"That seems farfetched to me. Maybe the money was her husband's. Did you think about that?"

Nah, who would ever think that? What did this Barnet think—that this was my first rodeo?

43

LUCA

SIGN OF THE CROSS MADE, I HELD MY BREATH UNTIL THE wheels touched ground. I got an immediate boost just by getting back home. I'm not sure how it works, but sitting for six hours drains you. And to pile it on, that six-hour ride plus the three-hour time difference killed an entire day. Anxious to follow up on what LAPD Detective Alonzo had dug up, I wondered if this was a case-breaker.

Alonzo, who looked to be in his mid-forties, surprised me. As soon as we met, I put him down as strange and distant. But he proved me wrong and turned out to be a good guy and an even better cop. Alonzo cared, and you couldn't ask for more than that.

The information he uncovered would go a long way to keeping Morgan off my back. It was surprising he didn't put up a stink when I mentioned going to Los Angeles. Deplaning, I thought it had to be that he was hoping to pin the murder on an outsider.

Vargas was picking me up. *Man, what a difference from LAX*, I thought as I made my way through the terminal. Regional Southwest was bright, airy, and had a relaxed feel.

It's not like I've been everywhere, but the L.A. Airport had a strong smell of jet fuel to go along with an aging structure. Who knows, the smell might have something to do with their lack of humidity and rain.

Vargas pulled up in a dark blue Explorer. I flung my overnight bag on the back seat and hopped in. She said, "Good trip, huh?"

Nodding, I said, "Glad to get home, though. We have a ton of transplants, but most of them don't come with their problems. But in L.A.? Everyone out there's got a story why they went out there. I can tell you, they may have better weather than where they came from, but those clowns still got the same problems."

"They don't call it La La Land for nothing."

I realized I didn't just miss home, I missed Vargas. "You ain't kidding, Mary Ann."

"On the phone you said you've got a new line on Barnet."

"Get this, Alonzo has a sister who was hoodwinked by some Brazilian on Match.com. This guy feigned interest in her and said he was coming to see her. Then at the last minute he gave her some bullshit about a visa and said he needed twenty thousand or he couldn't leave Brazil."

"Don't tell me she sent it."

I nodded. "Hard to believe that shit actually happens."

"I know, but it looks like Alonzo had a special motivation to help run this down."

"No doubt. He went much further than any cooperating officer since I got my badge. This Detective Alonzo, he was a little weird, but he picked up what we were digging for. Anyway, like I had said, Barnet was brought in for filming at least two women he was having affairs with."

"Arrested twice?"

"Yeah, but the women dropped the charges."

"Both of them?"

"Yeah, that's what bothered Alonzo. He could've left it at that but instead worked the edges. He tracked down a woman, Nancy Grillo. She's not in the same category as Boggs, but still has a fair amount of dough."

"She said Barnet tried to blackmail her?"

"No, but Alonzo thinks something's there."

"How come?"

"She and Barnet were a thing for a couple of months, kinda like Boggs. Then, according to one of her friends, Barnet filmed them having sex, just like he did with Marilyn."

"Okay, but that doesn't tell me much."

"Here's the thing, right after she told her friend about it, she disappears."

"Disappears?"

"She upped and left. Eventually, she sold her house and all. She would stay in touch with friends but never say where she was. After Barnet left Los Angeles, she let her friends know she had moved to Vail."

"You talked to her?"

"No, she's in Shanghai, not getting back for another ten days. Alonzo thinks she may open up to me."

"And why is that?

"Hey, can we just say it's my style?"

She frowned. "If you say so."

I was hoping she would say something nice. "I'm not with the LAPD. She doesn't have to worry about getting brought into anything out there or her home turf in Vail."

"But if we need her to testify?"

"I'm betting if we get something from her we'll crack Barnet."

44

LUCA

I TRACKED DOWN SANCHEZ'S LAWYER, WHOSE COMBATIVE approach had softened. Overloaded with cases, he agreed to let me see his client on the condition that I record the interview and immediately send him a copy.

Sanchez was outfitted in zebra-colored prison garb and a scowl. The corrections officer chained him to the gray steel table and retreated to a corner of the room.

"Where's my lawyer?"

I loosened my tie and opened the first button. "Stuck in court."

"We got nothing to talk about without him."

"He agreed to this get-together." I pulled out the authorization slip his lawyer had signed and handed it to him.

Sanchez looked at it. "How do I know this ain't no trick?"

"Believe it or not, you see those little cameras up there? Everything is documented, isn't that right, Officer?

The corrections officer confirmed, and we got underway.

"You and Mrs. Boggs got along?"

"I just worked there. I didn't know the lady."

"You only stole a couple of pieces of jewelry."

"Three rings and a necklace, that's all."

"But there were hundreds of pieces of jewelry there. All of them extremely valuable and you want me to believe that all you stole were just four pieces."

"It's true, that's all I took."

"And why was that? Why did you overlook such a treasure chest? You could've been set for life pawning all that jewelry."

"I didn't want to get caught. I just needed some money to help my mother."

"That's very noble of you, but there's something I'm interested in. With so many things to choose from, how did you choose what pieces to steal?"

"They were on a shelf."

"Did you know that the red cocktail ring you took was Mrs. Boggs' favorite?"

He shook his head.

"That it was a ring her father had given her and the only one that she cherished?"

"I don't know anything about that."

"You expect me to believe that choosing her favorite ring was completely random?"

"It's true, I swear."

"How quaint, you swearing to it. But Mrs. Boggs was a person with unlimited resources, with over two million dollars' worth of jewelry, and the piece you took is the only piece she considered irreplaceable. How does that sound to you?"

"But that's what happened."

"You said you didn't know Mrs. Boggs. Is that correct?"

"Yeah, I didn't know the lady."

"But you were seen speaking with her."

He paused for a microsecond. "It was nothing. Just like hello, how are you doing?"

"Really? Just normal everyday pleasantries?"

He nodded. "That's right."

"You know what I think? I think you were trying to extort a cool fifty grand from your employer."

"What are you talking about?"

"You knew that Mrs. Boggs was attached to a ring her daddy had gotten for her, and you stole it. You couldn't keep your greed in check and took a couple of other pieces as well. With the ring missing, you went to her, maybe tried to play the hero and said you could get the ring back for her if she paid you fifty thousand in cash."

He wagged his head. "No, that's crazy."

"You think so? Then why did Marilyn Boggs have fifty thousand in the very bedroom you burglarized? The cash had to have been put there after the theft or you would have taken that. Tell me, what other reason would Mrs. Boggs have for having that kind of money in her bedroom?"

"I dunno. I swear."

"Raul, I want to believe your claim that you didn't know any of this. But there's a little problem."

"What problem? It's true."

"It would ring truer if you didn't have a record for extortion and blackmail. See," I held his rap sheet, "you've got experience playing this game, and like before, you're gonna get nailed for it."

"I'm done talking. Take me back to my cell."

45

LUCA

THIS WAS THE SECOND TIME IN WEEKS I WAS OUT WEST. I checked the weather for Vail before I left, and it said a high of 41 and a low of 26, but the rental car said it was 74. Taking the long access road out of Denver International Airport, I was submerged in a postcard; snowcapped mountains reflected the sun against a bright blue, cloudless sky. Not a palm tree in sight, but it was pretty and warm.

Climbing up Route 70, the pine and aspen-covered mountains grew larger as the valley and its highway shrunk, and the temperature dropped under 60. Passing through the first of several old mining towns, my ears popped. A light snow that had begun falling stopped as I exited the Eisenhower Tunnel.

The sun began playing hide-and-seek with the Rockies and I turned up the heat. The temperature dropped under 50 and the plow piles grew. Homes seemed to be perched in places that were unreachable by car. How did they get to them with all the snow? These houses were big and had walls of glass, just like in Florida. I'd have to make sure I picked up a real estate magazine to see what the market was like out here.

Passing the exit for Vail, I headed for the Holiday Inn located in Avon, where room rates were a quarter of the prices in Vail Village. The heaviest jacket I owned was an old parka I kept around to use when I went to New Jersey. I threw on a sweatshirt emblazoned with the Naples Surf Club and pulled the parka over it.

The sun had disappeared and I slowly made my way on the slick roads. I could see thousands of sparkling lights as I approached Vail Village. After parking, I walked toward what looked like the center of the village. The place looked like Christmas Town itself. Walking over a covered bridge, I half expected to be greeted by elves.

The streets were filled with skiers and snowboarders in various states of festivity. It was easy to find Pepi's Bar and Restaurant. The orange-colored building seemed to be at the epicenter of Vail Village. Pepi's outdoor patio was packed, with a line of hopefuls sipping beers as they waited for a table. I was more hopeful than all of them combined and didn't have to wait, as Nancy Grillo had reserved a table under my name.

The hostess showed me into the Antler's Room, which looked like it belonged in The Sound of Music. Was I in Colorado or Austria? Unfinished chairs carved out of pine were set around tables covered with checkered tablecloths. Beer steins, numbering in the hundreds, lined the shelves and the waitstaff were costumed in lederhosen outfits. The music was either German or Austrian and the atmosphere was celebratory.

After ordering a beer, I crowd watched. Waiters were delivering food that seemed too fancy for the setting. I browsed the menu. It had a ton of game dishes on it and was pricey but with the time difference I was starved. Nancy Grillo wasn't due for another forty-five minutes. By then I'd be bombed without food.

I wasn't brave enough to order the Hungarian Goulash, so I opted for a bowl of the pea soup that had frankfurters in it. It was excellent and did the trick. Ordering my third brew, a bird of a woman headed in my direction. She was wearing a tailored hat of fur that matched her boots and a black suede coat.

I rose but she motioned for me to sit and peeled off her jacket. She was almost the same size as Marilyn Boggs. As she took off her hat I expected a pixie haircut, but she had her golden hair piled at the top of her head.

"Thank you for agreeing to meet with me. I understand your skepticism, but you can trust me."

She was expressionless. "My privacy is important to me. I don't enjoy being in the spotlight."

Well, if that was the case, she picked a hell of a town to live in. "Believe me, you have nothing to worry about. As I told you, all I'm looking for is background information on John Barnet."

I saw her flinch at the sound of his name.

A waiter stopped by our table and took her order for a glass of Riesling.

Nancy lowered her voice. "I have a good life here. It was an adjustment, but you'd be surprised how real the full-timers in the valley are. There's a considerable amount of flash during the ski season, but the locals are down-to-earth and took me in like one of their own." She flashed a quick smile before it melted into a frown when she said, "I can't start over again."

I leaned forward. "I assure you, Nancy, whatever you

share with me stays between us. It will only be used to help steer my investigation in the right direction."

"What has *he* done this time?"

"That's the thing, we're really not sure."

"He's a very deceptive, dangerous person. I'd put him out of my mind until that Los Angeles detective began calling me."

"I'm sorry to have to dredge all this up, but it's important."

A waitress sidled up to our table and recited the specials but there were no takers. Nancy ordered the Tuna Sashimi and I took her suggestion, ordering the rack of lamb.

"I don't want to push you. Believe me, I'm grateful to be here. But could you tell me a little about yourself? What do you do?"

She explained that her grandfather was a pilot and had owned a flight school in Orange County only thirty-five miles from Los Angeles. The location and runways made it a perfect choice for a secondary airport and Orange County bought it, renaming it John Wayne Airport. She said her grandfather and father invested the money in real estate and that she was the only beneficiary of the trust they formed.

It was clear, though I didn't want to rub it in, that Barnet targeted her. "I assume Bar—"

She shook her head.

"Sorry, I assume he knew of your family's financial situation?"

She nodded.

"How did you happen to meet him?"

As I digested the fact they had met at a charity event, a cheery waiter delivered our plates and we, or I, dug in. Either I was very hungry or it was the best rack of lamb I ever had. I looked around and saw at least two people holding them like lollypops, giving me the permission I sought to grab and gnaw away.

A millisecond after I put the last bone down, a waiter appeared and cleared the table.

"That lamb was great. Thanks for suggesting it."

Nancy smiled. It helped melt her awkwardly proportioned face.

"I hate to get back to all this, but." I threw my hands up.

"It's okay."

I leaned forward and spoke with the hushed tone of an undertaker. "A friend of yours mentioned that he took some pictures of you that you did not consent to."

She pulled her lips in. "Unbelievable."

"You could have pressed charges."

"And get dragged through the press? No, thank you."

"So, you decided to take off? Not that you can exactly call going to Vail running away."

She shrugged and studied her hands.

There was something there. "I get it, but the timeline confuses me. The camera thing happened about three months before you left Los Angeles."

Nancy shifted in her chair. "I—I had to make arrangements."

"Did you ever lend or give money to him?"

She bit her lip but was saved by a waiter bearing dessert menus. We ordered coffees and she suggested I try the strudel. I mean how could you not in this place?

"Did he ask for a loan?"

"I still can't believe how gullible I was."

"How much?"

She shook her head. "First, it was ten thousand, but the next time it was twenty."

"You gave it to him?"

"Yes, but I told him that was it. He asked again and again but I held my position."

"How were things going in the relationship when you held the line?"

She chortled. "That was the thing; he totally compartmentalized things like nothing happened. But me, I was very troubled by it and tried to put space between us."

Our coffees and my strudel appeared and I had a hard time not digging in. I had to keep the MO going and told myself the strudel would be my reward. I took a sip of coffee, leaned in and took a chance.

"I'm sure you're not aware, but that was his modus operandi. And when a woman refused to play along, he'd film them and blackmail them. Is that what happened?"

She nodded and hung her head. I prayed she wouldn't start crying. "I was afraid of him. He never said it directly, but he always insinuated that he'd hurt people in the past, and he was talking physically. I probably should've reported it, but I was scared and took off."

"There's absolutely nothing to be ashamed of. Frankly, I'm proud of you. Most women would've caved, but you did the right thing."

"You think so?"

"I know so. You told him to go to hell and look where you're living. You ask me, Vail is a zillion times nicer than L.A. Besides, look at this strudel, will you?"

Strudel aside, when I stepped into the night's frigid air, the hairs in my nostrils tingled. They were freezing together! It forced me to reconsider my comment about Vail versus Los Angeles.

46

LUCA

AFTER APPEALING TO TWO SEPARATE COURTS TO INVALIDATE
our subpoena, Verizon finally caved and complied with our
request for access to Barnet's cloud account. With Marilyn
dead, the video of her was a lot less valuable, and I figured he
probably would have deleted it from his phone. Besides,
asking or getting a subpoena to examine his actual phone
would alert him.

The geeks down in electronic forensics pulled down eight
videos. Barnet should have gone to work for that sleazebag
who owned *Hustler* magazine. I had zero interest in this
pornography and went straight to the newest one. I did a
double take. It said it was over twelve minutes long. Even
though it was a legitimate part of the investigation, I got up
and closed my office door before hitting play.

Beyond uncomfortable, I stopped it after just a minute
and twenty seconds. It was undeniably Marilyn Boggs, and if
she didn't consent to it, the video would clearly violate the
revenge porn law, providing it had been posted to the Internet. I wondered if having it go to his cloud account qualified

as a post because the search the geeks conducted came back with nothing.

It wasn't surprising. Barnet wasn't looking to embarrass these women; as best I could tell, he wanted their money. Still, if this was New York or Jersey and we got one of the other women to file a complaint that the filming was not consensual, we could lock his tanned ass up.

It was something to pursue, as it would get Barnet to regret his perverted ways, whether he killed Boggs or not.

WATERSIDE SHOPS WAS BUZZING with shoppers and sightseers, but it was quiet inside Barnet's Wine & Spirits. A redheaded sales girl smiled at me when I entered.

"Can I help you find anything this afternoon?"

I said, "Not just yet, thanks."

"Take your time, let me know if I can help. My name's Carla; I'm the assistant manager."

Heading to the Italian section, I noticed the racks were not fully loaded. There were a dozen slots in each row but only half were occupied. They were packed the last time I was in.

Scooting over to the French and the California sections, I noted they were similarly light on inventory. Was this normal? Wines were seasonal, and he did just have a big sale. Maybe the new vintages hadn't arrived yet.

Circling through the store, I passed the saleslady again and she said, "You sure I can't help?"

"As a matter of fact, I was looking for a wine, John, I think he's the owner, suggested."

"What was the name of the wine?"

"That's the thing, I can't remember."

"Red, white?"

I threw my hands up. "I know it sounds crazy, but he made a couple of suggestions that seemed to be great."

"John's a big fan of Bordeaux. Was it a Bordeaux?"

"No. That I'd remember. Is he around by any chance?"

She nodded. "He's in his office. Let me see if he's free."

Standing off to the left, I watched Barnet tuck his shirt in as he hustled out of his office. Surveying the store as he walked, he saw me and paused before forcing a smile.

"Good to see you again. Carla said you were looking for a wine I had mentioned. The last time you were in, did I recommend a Barolo?"

"I don't think so. You were doing a tasting in the back room with two women."

He smiled. "Just two?"

"Yeah, I remember it was ninety bucks a bottle, and I said it was too expensive for me, that I'd never know the difference."

"Oh yeah, I remember now. We were tasting a Burgundy. And don't sell your palate short. As you drink more wines you'll easily pick up the differences in them."

I chuckled. "If it means I got to spend more on a bottle, I'm not sure I want that kind of sense."

"Let's go to the Burgundy section."

He pointed to a multicolored map over a rack of wine.

"It's important to understand there are various regions within Burgundy. The wines are very different from each other, even within the sub-regions themselves."

There were a lot of names, starting with Cote, but the only name I recognized was Chablis. This guy was really into this stuff. He talked nonstop for fifteen minutes until I slid a bottle out of one of the slots.

"Sorry, I can get carried away at times, but it's because I believe in the importance of terroir. That's an excellent bottle you've got, but for you, it may be a bit on the expensive side at seventy-nine ninety-five."

I slid the bottle back in.

"Take a look at this one." Barnet took a bottle out of a bin. "It's by a well-known producer, Louis Jadot, whose wines are readily available. I think we have at least fifteen wines of theirs. This is a Cote de Nuits." Barnet pointed to the map. "That's the red region at the top. It's what's known as a village wine. This one has nice flavors of darker cherries with a hint of strawberries. It's medium-bodied with good depth. It's not terribly complicated, but I believe it's a great introduction, especially at under thirty dollars."

Hearing the description, I wanted to pop the cork right then and there. "Sounds real interesting. I appreciate you respecting my budget. We don't make much money in my line of work."

"My pleasure. Look, take a bottle of this as well. It's a Volnay from Beaune, which is south of where the Jadot is from."

As I took both bottles from him, Barnet said, "Let me know how you like them. We've got plenty of affordable wines, so tell your friends about us. I've got to run. Thanks again for coming in."

"Can you hang on a minute? I've got a couple of questions."

"I really don't have time today."

"It'll be quick."

Barnet took the bottles back and marched to the counter. "Ring these up. We're going into my office for a minute. I want to show him an aerial view of Burgundy."

As we entered his office, Barnet made reference to a photograph hanging on the wall behind his desk. It was a picture taken on an angle of a vineyard in Burgundy where the rows of vines followed the contour of the rolling hills. There wasn't a soul in sight and the image exuded natural beauty.

Barnet sat behind a desk with at least a dozen bottles of wine in a semicircle. Three glasses and a corkscrew were ready to be deployed.

"You doing a tasting?"

He nodded. "Was just about to when you came in."

"That's a lot of wine."

Barnet reached below the desk and came up with a bucket. "That's what this is for. I taste and spit."

"What do you do with the rest of the bottle?"

He shrugged. "If it's something I'm interested in carrying, I make sure to have the staff taste it. That way they have an understanding of the wine, otherwise it goes down the sink."

Nodding, I realized there really was a world of difference between a place like this and buying wine at Publix, like I usually did. It would be fun to keep talking about wine, but it was time to move on.

"By the way, I noticed empty spots in the racks. Seems like there's a lot less inventory."

"We've got a ton of wine coming in. Frankly, I don't know where I'm going to put it all."

"Sounds good. Look, I wanted to go over a couple of items with you concerning Marilyn Boggs."

Barnet stiffened, pulling his hands off the table.

"You had said that her favorite wine was Sauvignon Blanc."

"Yes, she enjoyed that as well as the white wines of Bordeaux, which are made of Semillon and Sauv Blanc."

"But on the day of her murder we found an open bottle of pinot noir on the kitchen counter."

"Maybe she was having it with the person who did it."

My ears perked at the 'who did it.' Was it his emotional attachment to Marilyn that prevented him from facing the facts she was stabbed to death? Or was it a subconscious side-step to soften the violent act? Before I could say anything, he added, "It was probably Gideon."

"He likes pinot noir?"

"I think so."

"Your last time together with Marilyn, did you have sexual intercourse?"

"Come on, Detective, isn't that a bit personal?"

"Answer the question, please."

Barnet wagged his head. "Yes."

According to the autopsy, he was lying. Tucking the deception into a mind file, I moved on.

"Gideon Brighthouse said the two of you were arguing when he came into the house the afternoon of her murder."

"Arguing? No, he's got it wrong."

"What was it then?"

"I can't remember what we were talking about when he came in, but we certainly weren't arguing."

"Are you sure about that?"

"Detective, I hope you're not trying to imply that we were arguing and . . . well, you know."

"I don't deal in implications; my world is all about the evidence."

47

LUCA

I WAS CHATTING WITH A PATROLWOMAN WHO HAD JUST JOINED the department when Vargas stuck her head out of our office door.

"Hey Frank! Come here."

The new hire was cute; was Vargas jealous?

"What's up?"

"Just heard from George King."

"Who?"

"He worked with Brighthouse on Senator White's reelection. He finally returned, like, my tenth call."

"And?"

"He claims Brighthouse has temper issues. Said he was erratic at times and that he even saw him hit his wife."

"What? What exactly did he say?"

"It was right when the pay-for-play stuff came out on White. There was a small gathering for bundlers—"

"Bundlers?"

Vargas nodded. "They're people who not only heavily donate to a campaign but also go out and get other donors to support the campaign. Anyway, it was up at Fleming's Steak, and right before they were about to attend, Marilyn Boggs somehow got wind of the news about White. King said it was just the three of them left in the office and that Marilyn didn't want to go to the dinner. Brighthouse insisted that she had to go and they started arguing. King was right there, became uncomfortable and went to his office. After a few minutes, King came out and saw Marilyn heading for the door when Gideon grabbed her arm, spinning her around. Marilyn lost her balance and crashed into a photocopy machine. But instead of cooling things off, Gideon got back in her face. King jumped in the middle and broke up the fight, saying he believed Marilyn was in danger and that Gideon had totally lost control."

I was shocked; Brighthouse seemed reserved, almost meek. "He got physical with her?"

"According to King. He also said Brighthouse was prone to anger when the campaign started going south. Told me Brighthouse said, a number of times, that he wanted to kill the guy at Fox who broke the story."

"Words may establish patterns, but if we locked up everyone who said out of anger they wanted to kill someone, we be patrolling empty streets. What needs following up is the physical abuse aspect. But remember, there's no history of him being violent."

"This is a high-powered family. Who knows if there were any cover-ups? They could've paid someone or multiple people to keep quiet. Those agreements are sealed."

"I know money can buy silence, but there's always a whisper, a willingness to look the other way that seeps out. In this case we've got zippo indication he was violent."

Vargas said, "Remember, those agreements are secret, sealed by a court."

"And the only way to keep a secret between two people is when one of them is dead."

Vargas smiled. "As soon as 'secret' came out of my mouth, I knew you were gonna invoke that Lucaism."

"Lucaism, I like that. Maybe I'll start a blog with that name."

"Seriously, we need to ask Brighthouse about this. I'll reach out to Gerey to set it up."

"Okay, you know it might be worth running back over the campaign contacts, see if this guy King had an ax to grind with Brighthouse."

"Sure. We've got to check on the drugs he's taking. Maybe they're related to this. Why don't you ask the pharmacology department at Gulf Coast University? They'll know if they can make you violent."

Another Vargas gem. "Good idea, but the campaign thing happened before Brighthouse started getting his panic attacks."

"Still worth checking."

"I got it covered."

CLOSING AN EMAIL, I said, "Is this guy kidding me? Gerey wants us to submit our questions in writing. Says it'll be too much for his client to come in. Gerey is claiming Brighthouse is under too much stress."

"He should be, he's a suspect in his wife's murder."

"I don't know, Vargas. These damn lawyers think they rule the world. But you know what? They can't push Luca around. Gerey wants to play games? Fine, now I'm gonna send a couple officers out to Keewaydin and drag Gideon's sophisticated ass down here."

"Hold on, Frank. It might be a good idea to run all of this by Morgan. We don't need Gerey running to him."

She was right, again. "This bureaucratic bullshit is killing me."

"You want me to go see Morgan?"

I nodded. "He certainly likes you a helluva a lot more than me."

"WHAT'D HE SAY?"

"It's a good compromise, kinda meet in the middle. He called Gerey, who said getting both Crowley and him to come in wouldn't be for two weeks."

"Who the hell is running this show?"

"Hold on, Frank. The interview is set for the Boggs apartment on Fifth Avenue, and Crowley won't be there."

"What's Morgan, like Solomon now?"

"It's a good setup, Frank. Brighthouse will be off the island and out of his comfort zone."

"We'll see. I'm taking bets he either comes in stoned or has another panic attack."

"Let's hope not. Hey, you get anything on the drugs from the university?"

"Sorry, it came in this morning. I got distracted with this Gerey bullshit."

"That's okay. What'd they say?"

"Basically, that one rarely gets violent when having a panic attack, unless you're in their way when they want to escape, but the shrink also said that in some patients the interaction of drugs can cause violent outbursts."

48

A SALESCLERK KNOCKED ON BARNET'S DOOR AND SAID, "John, there's a Mr. Farnham on one. He's upset, something about a futures order."

"Can't you give it to Bridgette?"

"Uh, you fired her."

"Give me the damn call!"

"Mr. Farnham. How are you? . . . I understand, sir, I had to let my store manager go. . . . Yes, Bridgette. She made a real mess of the futures program, and it's going take me a bit of time to sort things out. You can't believe how she mixed up all the orders. . . . I promise to get back to you in ten days, max. . . . Ten is an outside number. I've got to get in touch with all the chateaus. I just can't trust the records she kept. . . . Thank you for understanding, sir. I should have known better letting someone else handle the orders, but I can tell you, it will never happen again."

Barnet opened the futures spreadsheet. Column C displayed the total case count—nearly eighty cases of the upcoming Bordeaux vintage were sold. Scrolling to E, he noted the total sold was for $113,450.00, and in column F, the seventy-five- percent deposit money taken in was $85,087.50.

The wine was due to start arriving in five months. His problem was twofold: he'd only ordered a bit more than half the wine he sold futures for, and all the money was gone. If this blew up he'd lose the store, along with everything else he had.

Barnet knew he'd also have to move again, but where? Chicago was a good wine town, but the weather was terrible. What about Scottsdale? Good weather, but it wasn't a wine town and wasn't near the water. The prospect of a move made him call a buddy to go out with that night. Barnet was going to go trolling for another lifeline and had a couple of cougars in mind.

It was the first time Bridgette had been in the sheriff's office. The security had frightened her, but, once inside, she was surprised at how quiet it was. The outer wall of the second floor was ringed with offices. Mirroring the one she was in, each had a large plate glass window looking over the bullpen area, which was lined with clumps of desks facing each other. Many of the desks were empty, but those that weren't were manned by a mix of uniformed and undercover officers.

Detective Wiley said, "Okay, ma'am. Why don't you tell me why you're here?"

"John Barnet is ripping off his customers. He should be in jail. He makes it seem—"

"Slow it down, ma'am. Are we talking about the John Barnet from Barnet's Liquors?"

"Yeah, the one that owns the Waterside store. How do you know him?"

"What are you alleging he is up to?"

"It's not alleged, he's doing it. He's taking money for futures orders but not buying the wine to satisfy the orders."

"Futures?"

"In the wine business, you have the opportunity to buy a new vintage before it's released. You see, the wine sits in barrels for a long time before it is bottled and released for sale. So, if you buy in advance you get a better price and a guarantee you will get these highly allocated wines."

"And how do you know Barnet is not going to deliver the wines that were ordered?"

"I worked as his store manager for almost three years."

After making a note, Wiley said, "Take it slowly and explain what you believe is going on."

"We'd never gotten into the futures business before. Bleu Cellar had a lock on the market, but we were slow this summer and John came to me about starting a futures campaign to get some traffic. We got orders but he wasn't happy with it and wanted more. Anyway, we had over a hundred thousand dollars in orders, but I know he didn't order all the wine."

"You know this how?"

"I was the one who did the ordering, and to make matters worse, he sold wine futures for producers who had cut him off because he was way behind in paying them."

"Isn't it possible he could buy the wine from a secondary source?"

"It's possible, but he'd lose money on it, if he could get it in the first place."

"What do you think he did with the money, if he didn't order all the wine?"

"It mostly went to cover the bills. The store really never got the traction he thought it would. You ask me, it was in the wrong location and the rent is out of control. Waterside is filled with all high-end designer shops. It's a different crowd."

"You believe Barnet was under monetary pressure and used some of the money he took in to cover his operating expenses?"

"Yeah, like a Ponzi scheme. So, should I be filing a complaint or something?"

"It's not that simple. First, if you didn't participate in buying the futures, you don't have standing to file a complaint. We need one of the customers to file."

"No problem, how many do you want?"

"In time, as the other problem is that no one has been defrauded yet."

"But they will be."

"Maybe, but Barnet could buy the wine he needs to deliver or even just refund the customers their money."

"Where's he going to get the money for that?"

"That's up to him. When are the buyers supposed to get the wine they ordered?"

"Some of it is due to arrive in the States in five months or so."

"We'll have wait and see how this plays out and whether Barnet is able to satisfy the buyers, one way or another. At this point, it's too early to do anything. A crime has not been committed."

"That's crazy. I'm telling you, John Barnet is a very dangerous man. He told me he beat up a guy so bad he ended up in intensive care."

"When was this?"

"I'm not sure, but it was when he was in Los Angeles."

"That's way out of our jurisdiction, ma'am."

"Yeah, well, he did the same thing to a bill collector right here in Naples."

"Tell me about that."

"There was this guy, I think his name was Vincent Ropo or something like that, and he would always come to the store and try to collect the money Barnet's owed to a Chilean winery. John wouldn't pay, saying the wine was tainted, but I knew he was lying. He didn't have the money. Anyway, this Vincent guy would come at least twice a week. Then, all of a sudden, he stopped coming."

"Maybe Barnet paid the bill or the winery wrote the loss off."

Bridgette shook her head. "I asked John what happened, and he smiled, like, so wickedly, I knew he'd attacked the poor guy."

49

LUCA

I hung up the phone just as Vargas swept into the office and said, "I think it might be time to drag Barnet in for a chat."

"Why? What changed?"

"That was Barnet's old store manager. She said Barnet doesn't have the money to replenish stock. He's into a couple of distributors for some big wood and behind in the rent."

"She the one who wanted to file a fraud complaint?"

"Yeah, she still doesn't understand why we're letting this entire wine futures fraud play out. I told her the same thing Wiley told her—Barnet may be planning, but he hasn't done anything yet."

"Just like Brighthouse?"

"I'll answer that for you as soon as I can. Right now, we know Barnet needs money—a perfect motivation for blackmail, wouldn't you say?"

"I'm sorry; I just don't get why Marilyn wouldn't fight back, especially with the firepower the Boggs have."

"It's all about the reputation. Who knows what else Barnet may have had on her?"

"But he didn't. We know from the Verizon records he only had one on her."

"He could've had it stored on a hard drive, a flash drive, or something."

"Look, I think this entire filming thing is disgusting, consent or not, but in today's world it might make a headline on a slow day."

"We're not dealing with normal people. You could be right, but it's what she thought, not what we or others think about it. Who knows, the old man probably has a section in the trust about it."

"You might be on to something, Frank. Maybe there is some kind of clause dealing with harming the family reputation or something."

"If so, the old man must've been some sort of narcissist. You think he really believed everyone was focused on the Boggs and what they did?"

"I'm sure it had to do with managing people's money and having a lily-white reputation, otherwise it'd be tough for people to hand their money over."

"People really have to stop worrying about what people think of them."

"I know. Say, before I forget, Assistant DA Lindsey called about Sanchez. He wants to know what's going on. Wanted to reach out to Immigration and have him deported rather than go to trial if we're not going to charge him with murder."

"What the hell is wrong with them? They know Sanchez is one of our major suspects in the Boggs case."

"That's what I told them. They're probably pushing to dispose of cases, knock down their backlog. Make their numbers look good."

50

LUCA

SETTING A COFFEE ON MY DESK, I PICKED UP A MARKER AND went to the whiteboard. I drew three circles and put either G, B, or S inside them.

"Let's start with Gideon." I wrote below the encircled G: Close to victim, found body, Motive - Money, Planned to kill, No criminal history.

"Anything else?"

Vargas said, "He is on medication, and they're the type of drugs that some people get violent on. Could've been a drug-induced rampage."

Adding *On meds* to the list, I took a sip of coffee and said, "Let's move on to Barnet for the moment."

Under B, I wrote: Close to victim, present day of murder, motive - revenge? - no record but evidence of attempted extortion.

Vargas said, "I don't buy the revenge angle. If anything, it could have been an argument that spun out of control. Maybe Barnet was threatening Marilyn to get her to pay and things spun out of control."

"They were arguing, according to Brighthouse, and

though Barnet said they had sex that afternoon, zero evidence of it came out of the autopsy."

Crossing out revenge, I inserted *argument/fight instead.* "There's nothing concrete, but Grillo and his store manager both believe Barnet has a violent side."

"Unless we get proof, it's just hearsay."

I said, "I know. Let's not forget pinot noir is Barnet's favorite wine."

"There's no evidence he was the one drinking the bottle found at the scene."

"You don't see it on the board, do you? Now, on to Sanchez." I wrote as I talked. "He was on the island the day of the murder. Admitted being in the house to steal her jewelry. Seen talking to Mrs. Boggs. Motive, if there was one, was to conceal his blackmailing, just like Barnet."

"And Sanchez has a serious criminal history before coming to the States."

Grabbing my coffee, I sat down. "Sticking with Sanchez, no doubt he's no choirboy. I just don't know if he had the smarts or balls to run a blackmail scheme."

"But don't forget it would have been a onetime thing. Once she paid whatever he asked to get the ring back, he'd have nothing to extort with. It's much easier than something ongoing."

"Probably, but who could he say took it and approached him?"

"He could say someone, maybe a gang member, knew he worked on the island and approached him."

"How would the thief know what to steal? With all that jewelry in the bedroom, he comes out with a couple of pieces and one of them is her favorite? I don't buy it."

"Who knew it was her favorite? Barnet and Brighthouse

had to know. You think there could be a connection with Sanchez and one of them?"

It was something I'd never considered. Vargas was becoming a better detective than I was.

"We're gonna have to take a look at that. But if it turns out to be Sanchez, I think he surprised her during the theft and panicked. Let's get back to Gideon for the time being. That he planned to kill his wife is irrefutable if not illegal. Did he stab her to death? He was on the island and found, or was that, reported, her body? His motive? To avoid divorce that would have left him like the rest of us. But he would get millions if she was dead."

"Sounds like our number one."

"He may be. I like this Barnet as much as I like going to the dentist. He's one sleazy, money-hungry bastard. We know he at least tried to blackmail a woman with the same profile as Boggs."

"And we know he was with her just hours before she was found dead. The captain of the yacht who ferried him back to the mainland said they left around three, which was earlier than normal."

"The question is why? Was it just a harmless argument? Why wouldn't he just say so?"

"It could've been about the money he was sucking out of her and he wanted to keep that quiet."

"Probably was, but it's a big leap going from blackmail to murder. It doesn't normally happen."

"Nothing about this case is normal."

"I'm not going to let this case be added to the two-hundred-thousand unsolved murders over the past sixty years."

FOR THE FIRST time in months, a nightmare featuring the Barrow case woke me, crushing another of my hopeful expectations. What did I expect? A kid killed himself because I didn't stop the effort to railroad him. Being green wasn't an excuse. I'd have to learn to live with it, like Vargas said. I knew she was right and swung my legs off the bed. The clock read 5:12, and my throat was bothering me. I went to the bathroom, and while waiting for the pee to flow, thought over the Boggs case. After relieving myself, I decided to make a cup of tea and read the entire case file.

After cutting a lemon and squeezing a half into my tea, I grabbed the six-inch Boggs file and sat down. The first document in it was the forensics report from the crime scene: a long list, identifying the what and where of a collection of hairs, fibers, latent prints, one shoe imprint, and the blood, all of which came from the victim.

The identities of the hair samples and prints were not surprising. Besides the victim, most of the hairs and fingerprints belonged to Gideon Brighthouse, John Barnet, and three housekeepers. I remembered my initial interest in an identified hair, but testing tied it to a man who delivered the flower arrangements each week.

The fiber report was a long list but nothing unusual stood out. If we had a firm suspect, we'd hopefully use it to tie his presence to the scene. It wouldn't be a clincher, just supporting evidence.

Drinking the last of my tea, I turned to the physical evidence collected at the scene: the empty wine glass and a nearly empty bottle of Kistler Pinot Noir. Who had drunk the wine? It was still undetermined. The only thing interesting about the Omega Juicer was Gideon's intention to use it as the delivery system for the mushroom poison.

The most important physical evidence we had was the

knife used to kill Marilyn Boggs. The report said it was made by Zwilling of Germany, and not surprisingly, expensive. Its black, wood handle had been wiped of prints, and its serrated edge was fourteen inches long. No wonder it went straight through the poor woman. The blood found on the knife belonged to Marilyn Boggs. I unclipped the photo of the knife and pleaded with it to speak to me.

Clipping the photo back, it hit me. I popped out of my seat and went to the counter where my lemon and knife lay. Sure enough, there was a drop of lemon juice that had slid off the knife onto the counter. I grabbed the case file and flipped back to the forensics report.

No drops of blood were found anywhere, including where the knife was found. The killer either had wiped it down or was wearing gloves. The blade was left untouched. He or she didn't rinse it either, as no traces of blood were found in the sink.

I checked the time; it was only 6:18. Damn, there were two full hours before I could scratch my itch.

51

LUCA

Medical Examiner Shields looked up from his monitor and shook his head.

"I don't have time, Frank."

"This will be quick, I promise."

"You know, you always say that, and it never is."

"It's important, Doc."

Looking at his watch, he said, "You've got five."

"Thanks. Serrated knives have all those little edges, so if one was used to stab someone, when they pull it out, would it take blood with it?"

"There are many factors, starting with the arc used to stab. If the victim was on the ground or significantly reclined, gravity would play a role."

"Okay. How about a normal, smooth blade versus a serrated one when used in a stabbing? What's the blood-drip difference?"

"Standing, sitting? Deep puncture or not?"

"Standing. The attacker is taller than the victim, and it's as deep a wound as could be made, straight through the chest, like in the Boggs case."

"A long, serrated blade was used in that. Are we talking about that killing?"

"Yes."

"I'm generalizing, Frank, as even the clothing the victim wears has a role—"

"But she had a light blouse on; you saw it."

He nodded. "It was somewhat unusual that no blood drippings were found at the crime scene. A flat knife would tend to have the blood on the blade run off, generating a larger, blob-like drip. A serrated edge has many points of contact. It actually has less contact area than a smooth blade, and the contact points are finer, meaning less blood would collect on each contact point."

"What about any dripping?"

"There is a tendency to produce smaller droplets of blood."

"And where would theses droplets fall?"

"This is an inexact science, Frank. The force and speed of the thrust and removal would play a large role in where the blood, if any, would fall. And we haven't mentioned the angle of the stabbing."

"Can you stand, Doc?"

"What?"

"Humor me a second and come around."

As Shields came around his desk, I grabbed a pencil off it.

"Doc, you're a bit taller than me, so take this pencil and pretend it's a serrated knife. Now, Marilyn Boggs was stabbed right about here, severing her aorta. I would think that would generate a lot of blood."

"Naturally."

I bent my knees a little. "Hold the pencil near the eraser."

Grabbing the pencil, I guided his hand to where Marilyn had been stabbed.

"Okay, now envision pulling the blade out and do it with the pencil."

The coroner pulled the make-believe blade back sharply, and when it was by his ear I said, "Hold it! See where you are?"

The coroner relaxed and let his hand fall to his side. "Now, you want to know where a drop of blood could have gone? Assuming there was one."

"Exactly."

"Well, there wasn't any evidence of blood on the floor or cabinetry. It is possible that when the knife was yanked out," he put his fist by his ear, "a drop or drops of blood flew off the knife and onto the attacker."

"On his shirt?"

"No, I don't think so. As he pulled the knife out and toward him, during that arc, if something was falling off the knife, gravity would play a role. I think if it did happen at all, and it's a long shot, it would end up on his pants, or leg if he was wearing shorts."

"Thanks, Doc, you're a lifesaver."

"When you say that, do you mean again?"

As soon as I hit the parking lot, a text from Vargas came in. She had gone to see Sanchez, offering him a deal on the burglary charges if he could give us something tangible against either Barnet or Brighthouse. The setup was good but It didn't pan out, as Sanchez denied ever meeting Barnet and said he never spoke with Gideon other than a hello. Vargas believed him. There wasn't a connection, and out went the conspiracy theory.

SHERIFF MORGAN WAS GRUMBLING as Vargas and I entered his office, making me thankful she was with me.

"Good afternoon, Sheriff," Vargas said.

"Ma'am, Luca. You got something to brighten my day?"

I said, "We're exploring a way to bring the Boggs case to a conclusion, sir."

"It's about time." Beckoning with his hand, he said, "Tell me about it and make it quick. I've got some PR thing at Barron High School."

I said, "The crime scene had no blood besides what was on the floor beneath the victim and on the murder weapon itself. That's fairly unusual."

"You're just realizing this now?"

"No, no. It's not that it's unusual, but we need to explore the possibility that blood may have fallen onto the killer's clothes."

"And you don't think he discarded them?"

Vargas said, "It's possible, Sheriff, but the knife had a serrated edge, and they tend to produce tiny droplets of blood. Maybe the killer didn't even notice a tiny drop of blood got on him."

Morgan ran a hand over his flattop. "So, we're hanging our hat on, one, that a drop of blood fell on the attacker, and two, he or she didn't realize it? Sounds wishy-washy to me."

"It may be a long shot, but the coroner believes it's not only possible but likely."

Morgan rested an elbow on his desk. "Shields said that?"

I said, "Yes." And then walked it back a baby step. "In fact, we reenacted the stabbing multiple times, and he's of the opinion it's well within the realm of possibilities."

"So, you came here to seek a subpoena?"

Vargas said, "Yes, we'd like to request three."

"Three? That sounds a little greedy."

"We don't think so, sir. We have three possible suspects: John Barnet, he was there the day of the killing; Raul Sanchez, the jewelry thief, who's in custody; and Gideon Brighthouse."

"If I agree, what's the scope going to be?"

I said, "We're going to ask for all articles of clothing be taken and tested."

"You're going leave Mr. Brighthouse with nothing to wear, not even his underpants?"

"Vargas said, "Sir, we'd limit it to outer garments: shirts and pants.""

"What are they going to wear while you test?"

Vargas said, "Detective Luca and I discussed this at length, sir. Our plan is to take luminol with us when we execute the subpoena, that is, if you agree. Then, we'll spray five or six sets of clothing, and if they come up clean we'll leave them behind. After that, we'd move quickly to process the balance of clothing."

"I appreciate your consideration, Mary Ann, but did it occur to either one of you that someone like Gideon Brighthouse probably owns more clothing than the three of us put together? How are you going to process that volume of clothing, not to mention the others, quickly?"

I said, "We can work through Mr. Brighthouse's apparel first."

"You're going have Gerey all over me. Who knows, they may even go to the press with some nonsense we took all his clothes. There's got to be another way we can do this. Try the other two and see if you get a hit, make Brighthouse last."

"We considered that, but we're afraid if Brighthouse gets word of the testing, he'll destroy any evidence."

Morgan said, "That's if he hasn't already."

"We can put a blockade around Keewaydin, you know,

check everything that goes in and out, make sure there are no fires on the island—"

"God damn it, Luca, you think this is Venezuela or something?"

Throwing a crazy idea always makes the alternative look better. "Sorry, sir, but there's no easy way to do this."

Vargas said, "I'm afraid Detective Luca is right, sir. We're sorry to put you in a tight spot, but we feel it's a necessary course of action that can help us close the case quickly."

Morgan leaned back in his chair and put a cowboy boot on the edge of his desk. "I've got to roll this one around."

52

LUCA

No one on the team was in uniform. We had just stepped off the boat when I saw Gideon rise off a chaise. He looked in our direction and ran into the pool house.

"Let's move it! I don't want to give him a chance to destroy any evidence."

The six of us jogged toward the pool house. Pulling a slider open, we swarmed into the building like a SWAT team. Gideon wasn't on the ground floor. I took the stairs two by two and quickly knocked on a door before throwing it open.

Gideon was under the covers of his bed. Eyes closed, he was taking deep breaths, pushing his head into the pillow while inhaling and bending his head forward as he exhaled. Vargas squeezed into the doorframe saying, "It's okay, Mr. Brighthouse. Take it easy. No one is going to hurt you. You don't even have to answer any questions today."

We walked to his bedside. Gideon opened his eyes, looked at us, and clamped them shut. Scattered on the nightstand were three prescription bottles, caps off, and a glass of water. I picked them up: Valium, Xanax, and Ativan. Holding them out for Vargas to see, I motioned for her to speak.

"Gideon, how much medicine did you take?"

He kept breathing deeply, a good sign, as these drugs screw with your respiratory system.

"Do I need to call a doctor?"

He lay there, inhaling and exhaling like a Buddhist.

"If you don't tell me what you took, I'm going to have to take you to a hospital to make sure you're okay."

"Leave me alone, I'm trying to meditate."

"Did you take more than you're supposed to?"

"Why can't you just . . . leave me alone?"

"How many pills did you take?"

As he held out two fingers, I instructed the rest of the crew to search the lower level for any clothing.

"Are you sure?"

He nodded. "What do you want with me?"

I gave the subpoena to Vargas, who said, "We have a court order to examine your clothes."

He opened his eyes. "My . . . my clothes? Why?"

Vargas sat on the bed and explained what was going on and I went into the closet. It was like walking into the Wonderful World of Pastels. Almost everything this guy owned was in a pastel color. It was bizarre.

Spreading my arms as far apart as they could go, I pushed into a hanging section, grabbed a bunch of clothes and headed down the stairs. No way I was going get Gideon involved in choosing what he was going to wear.

I told the forensics guys to test the clothes. They opened their luminol kits, and I took the two other officers with me to the main house. I reminded them to leave all jackets and suits behind and to pack what qualified into black plastic bags.

It took only forty-five minutes for forensics to clear the first batch of clothes I had brought down. I asked them to keep testing until we were ready to depart.

An hour later, we left the island with less than I expected. Gideon may have been the king of pastels, but he was no clothes horse. In fact, he owned more pairs of shorts than pants and was curiously light on socks.

ONCE WE HIT THE MAINLAND, the forensics guys took the bags from Keewaydin. Vargas and I, and the two officers sped off for Barnet's place. A call came in right before we pulled up to the high-rise Barnet lived in; the group that had gone to Sanchez's had already finished inventorying what they took from his place.

Sitting on Gulf Shore Drive, the building had a good address, but it wasn't quite first class. Barnet was renting a two-bedroom on the second floor. We went into the lobby flashing our badges, explaining to the doorman why we were there. Vargas showed him the subpoena and he made a call to his boss. The doorman unlocked a drawer and fished out a set of keys. He tried to hand them over, but I asked him to accompany us as a witness.

We took the stairs, and when the doorman opened the door I headed straight for the master bedroom. Breezing past an unmade bed and a pair of underwear, I went to the closet. It was a walk-in. Scanning the half-filled closet, I looked for the blue pants and white shirt Gideon had remembered Barnet wearing. There were several that could be matches. I pulled a few out and looked them over but no dead ringers. I rehung them and surveyed the rest, a majority of the garments a form of linen. I checked some labels: "made in China" was printed on all of them. I'd have taken a bet right then that there wasn't an expensive one from Capri in the entire closet.

Before leaving the master suite, I went into the bathroom,

where a fraying towel hung over the bathtub. A hairbrush and toothpaste tube were all that was on the counter. I pulled the vanity draw open, and among the paraphernalia was a bottle of Just for Men. Finding it made me feel good.

The place had a lot of windows but no view, unless you liked looking straight into a mangrove hedge. I had wanted to look up a listing in the building but forgot. I wished I knew what a place like this traded for. The main room had a stylish-looking couch that screamed uncomfortable. A Lucite coffee table had a bowl of seashells on it and a coaster with a vine image. There was only one end table, and its lower half was stacked with copies of the *Wine Spectator*.

A half wall separated a dining area, where a black lacquer table supported a large bottle of wine. It was bigger than a magnum, empty, and had been signed by a bunch of people.

The galley kitchen had a sink with a couple of days' worth of plates in it. Sitting on the counter was a wine glass that looked the same as the one found in the Boggs home. I took a shot of it with my phone.

Looking around, I couldn't find any wine storage other than a small, under-the-counter job that was sitting in a closet. I don't know why, but I opened it and pulled two bottles out before I realized I didn't know what I was looking at. The doorman shadowed me, tapping away at his phone.

As the officers loaded the bags up, I went into the second bedroom. It was a mess. I knew that when you had no garage you needed somewhere to store your stuff, but this was ridiculous. Moving a couple of boxes out of the way, I got to the closet. Nothing in there but more boxes. Would he have put a blood-stained pair of pants in one of these boxes?

We'd be within our rights to search them, but the thought of going through all these boxes made me cringe. I wiped a finger across a couple of the boxes and came up with a dirty fingertip each time. Still uncertain what to do, I asked Vargas, and she agreed it didn't make sense.

I circled the apartment one more time before we left with three bags of clothing.

53

LUCA

THE FORENSICS LAB LOOKED LIKE A CLOTHING COLLECTION center for the Salvation Army. Two dozen black plastic bags, labeled with each respective owner's name, lined an entire wall. Two technicians worked methodically on a bag marked Brighthouse. They'd pull an article of clothing out, note identifying information into a tablet, and spray it with luminol. Then they slowly ran a black light over the garment, looking to see if a blue glow, signifying the presence of blood, appeared.

It was a tedious process and I considered asking Morgan to put another team on it. I was getting antsy, so I pulled off my hairnet and booties and left to grab a coffee. The cafeteria was quiet, and I scanned the real estate section someone had left behind. As I jotted down the particulars of a listing in Pelican Marsh, a patrolman sidled up to my table.

"Detective, you're wanted in the forensics lab."

"What's going on?"

"I don't know anything, was just told to find you."

Leaving my coffee behind, I bolted ahead of the officer to the stairs. Stumbling, I made my way down. Just before the landing, I tripped and was heading for a face plant. I reached out, snatching the handrail, steadying myself but overextending my shoulder.

I massaged my shoulder as I pushed through the lab's door into a small foyer for various forensic labs. I knocked on the window to get buzzed through, but the woman behind the partition pointed to her head. Pulling open a drawer in a stainless-steel cabinet, I put on a hairnet and booties and was buzzed into the bodily fluids lab.

"What's going on?"

"Got two hits."

"Two? On Brighthouse?"

"Yep." The technician grabbed a light. "They're over here."

I followed him to a steel table where a pair of pink pastel shorts and lime green pants were laid out. Two chalk circles had been drawn on each of their right legs. He turned the light on and held it over the circle on the pink shorts.

"See the glow."

"It's barely visible."

"I know, but that's what makes this an important tool. Over here there's a larger residue being detected."

He held the light over a mark on the pants.

"It looks like it could almost be a smudge."

"Possibly it was a drop that dripped down some before being absorbed."

"Or some blood that he tried to wipe off?"

"We'll find out soon enough."

"How soon?"

"The test to determine if it's human blood is quick. If it is, then we need to do a DNA match to see if it matches your victim."

THE TECHNICIAN'S definition of quick was vastly different than mine. Was he a Deep South boy? While we waited, Vargas and I tried to establish whether a string of late-night robberies were by the same gang. In the last month, eight convenience stores in the county had been held up, five of them using a gun, and the others with knives.

We studied the CCTV footage. Wearing ski masks, it was impossible to fix any facial features, though one seemed to indicate the thief had a mustache.

Vargas said, "It looks like we've got two or maybe three different perpetrators."

I didn't think so, but Vargas was on a roll and I wasn't, making me hesitant to disagree. Criminals who carried guns were in a class by themselves, and knife wielders almost never crossed over. "Could be."

"I wish we had another monitor to compare these against each other."

"Why don't we have the lab print some images, have them blow 'em up."

"Good idea."

Score one for Luca.

We went through the video again and made notes of the time stamps that offered the best comparative opportunities. Vargas took the information and video down to the lab and I leafed through a long memorandum on the opioid crisis. Collier had some addicts, and it sounds strange, but we were fortunate that most of those hooked were well-off and didn't need to resort to robbing to support their habit.

Two doctors, masquerading in East Naples as running pain clinics, had been busted, denting supply, but a pipeline from Miami had filled the void. The memo identified the gang they believed was behind the pill conduit, explaining they were using a combination of cars and boats to deliver the drugs.

These guys were clever, I thought, when my desk phone rang. The call from the lab was promising, raising my spirits. Scraping at a cuticle as I contemplated and extrapolated the news, Vargas came back. I glanced at the clock.

"It took four hours and we got a split decision. One of the stains was nothing more than horse radish."

"Horse radish? How did that show up as blood?"

"I said the same thing, but the lab said it triggers a false positive. Anyway, looks like the other stain is human blood. Now all we need is to see if it's from Marilyn Boggs."

MORGAN WANTED TO SEE ME, and I wish he'd asked before I got the call saying we had two chances at Brighthouse.

Wearing a scowl and one of his shoelace ties, Morgan grunted in the direction of a chair.

Before my tail hit the seat, he asked, "Gerey is threatening to file a complaint, calling it harassment."

"Maybe we should tell him we detected the presence of blood on two of his client's pants."

"Blood?"

"I shouldn't have spoken so soon. Sorry, sir. The forensics team has identified two garments with what they believe may be human blood."

"How damn long till they know?"

I was praying he wouldn't make a call to push and expose my fib. "Any minute now and we should know. I'm sure one of the two will be and that's all we need."

"No so fast, Luca. They'll need to run a DNA analysis to

determine who it came from. It could have been his own blood and probably is." He tapped a forefinger on the desk. "I'm getting a bad feeling about this. I shouldn't have let you talk me into it."

I wanted to remind him it was Vargas who swayed him, not me. "I don't know how much it helps, but we've still got about two dozen garments of Mr. Brighthouse's to check, along with Barnet and Sanchez."

"This is dragging on way too long, Luca. I need this case solved. I'm not leaving an open case for the next guy to deal with."

54

LUCA

THE ANXIETY WAS GETTING TO ME. I CONSIDERED SNEAKING into the forensics lab and moving the clock hands forward. That would be as crazy as I could imagine acting, though nothing like Gideon may have done.

The meeting was set for two p.m., but I was like a moth at a screen door at a few minutes after one. The message from John Forman said he had the Brighthouse results and a few other developments to discuss. I played back his message a handful of times but couldn't read between the lines. How come time never moved quickly when you wanted it to?

At ten to two I went outside, walked the length of the parking lot and came back. The big hand was still a hair shy of twelve. The receptionist had begun ignoring me a half-hour ago, so I knocked on the glass. She glanced at the clock and frowned before buzzing me through to the conference room.

I continuously circled the round table anchoring the windowless room, grabbing the back of a chair when dizziness crept up on me. The door opened and Forman came in, triggering the dizziness to flee.

He said hello, pulled out a chair, and put down a file on the lacquer table. "You're not going to sit, Frank?"

I fell into a chair and put my elbows on the table. "Your message, it left me hanging."

"Hanging? I don't remember saying anything mysterious. This case must be getting to you, Frank. And the sheriff too, it seems. He's been all over this one."

So, Morgan was sniffing, or barking around after all. All without telling his lead detective. It undermined my already shaky confidence.

"It's an important case, John. That's all. What do you have?"

"We've got a total of six hits."

"Wow. Six stains?"

"It's not unusual, considering the number of garments tested."

"What about the bloodstain found on the Brighthouse slacks?"

"DNA results match the victim, Marilyn Boggs."

"So that's it, we got Brighthouse."

"Not yet. We're running a test to date the stain. This blood could have been there for two years."

"I doubt it. How long is that going to take?"

"A week or so."

"You got to be kidding me."

"Do I look like I'm kidding?"

I shrugged. The answer was no; Forman had probably never told a joke in his entire life.

"In the meantime, we'll delve into the other stains."

"What are the odds, John? I mean, we have her blood on a major suspect's clothes."

"They were married, right? Who knows how or when it

got there. We've been down this path at least a dozen times since I've been here. That's why we do what we do."

He was right. I knew it, but the case felt like it was dragging. I could see the finish line, and now they're telling me I gotta make a pit stop?

"Fair enough. You said you had some other hits."

"Yes. All of them confirmed as human blood." He flipped open the file. "We found three stains on three pairs of pants identified as belonging to Sanchez. Two pairs of chino-type work pants, one on the right thigh and another on the left cuff. The third location was on the left shin area of a pair of jeans."

Trying to quickly calculate the odds any of it was from Boggs, I gave up and asked, "What about Barnet?"

"There were two human bloodstains identified from the Barnet inventory." He lifted a sheet of paper. "One on the right waistline of a shirt, and another on the right thigh of a pair of pants."

I lean forward. "What color?"

"Color?"

"Barnet's shirt and pants."

I GOT to my office an hour and changed earlier than I usually did. I figured with the results on the Boggs case coming in today, I'd better tidy up the paperwork on some other cases. Shadow-like, Vargas was five minutes behind me.

As she plunked down her pocketbook, she said, "Couldn't sleep last night."

"Who could?"

"What's that famous gut of yours telling you?"

I shrugged and she said, "Call the newspapers. Luca doesn't have an opinion."

I smiled. "I do, but it's conflicted. Let's hear yours."

"It's got to be Gideon Brighthouse. The quote, unquote, "loving husband" who plotted to kill his wife. It might have been Sanchez, as he returned to rob more jewelry and she caught him and things spun out of control. But the more I think about it, I always come back to Brighthouse."

"This is a seesaw for me with Barnet and Brighthouse. I don't think it was Sanchez, but I can't clear him because of his Mexican gang affiliation."

"But Barnet, he's a cretin, preying on women like he does. But it's a long leap from being a sleazy Romeo to a killer. At least with Sanchez, he has the violent gang history."

"True."

55

LUCA

PERCHED ON THE TOP STEP OF THE DUGOUT, I WAS AS READY as I ever was. The Boggs case had more turns than Lombard Street. This last go-round with the bloodstains was an episode of whack-a-mole.

No matter what Vargas said, I wasn't taking chances with our interrogation. I believed my pre-interview ritual worked, but whether that was in my head or not was beside the point. If I didn't make the suspect wait and squirm, it would undermine my confidence. For this interview, I'd decided rather than ballroom dancing and teasing information out, my tactical approach would be closer to mosh pit.

Vargas came down the hallway wearing a white frilly blouse I'd never seen. I wasn't sure it was appropriate for the task at hand. Then it hit me. Don't tell me she has another date tonight? It felt like things were moving too fast with this guy Damien. Was he Irish?

"You look nice."

Vargas smiled. "Coming from you, that's quite a compliment."

"What are you talking about? I say nice things to you all the time."

"It's okay, Frank. Just kidding. Relax."

I don't know why, but the words just spilled out of my big fat mouth. "Got another date with that Damien?"

She whipped her head around. "That Damien is none of your business."

I felt so small, I could play handball against the curb. "I'm sorry. I didn't mean it to come out that way."

"Apology accepted. You ready?"

Fact was, I wasn't ready. I needed a few minutes to collect myself. "If you don't mind, I need to go to the boy's room."

She smiled. "Take your time, Frank. I'll grab a coffee or something."

Heading to the bathroom, I wondered what that meant. She knew my situation about going pee-pee; I needed a lot of time. She couldn't be making fun of me, could she? Vargas was the most understanding person I'd ever met. And easy to unload to, never judging me. She couldn't mean anything else but not to hurry.

As I sat waiting for the pee to flow, I thought I'd surprise Vargas with something like a nice dinner at Bleu Provence to celebrate breaking the Boggs case. I heard her say she liked this place Damien took her. Yeah? Just wait till she goes to Bleu Provence.

HOLDING the door open for Vargas as we entered interview room two, I suppressed a smile. The room was perfect: windowless and the smallest space we had. As we took our seats, I nodded across the table. Vargas smiled that disarming smile of hers and clicked the record button. She recited the required formalities and looked my way.

I said, "When was the last time you had sexual intercourse with Marilyn Boggs?"

Shock broke out on his tanned face. "What kind of question is that?"

"Answer the question."

"It's none of your business."

"That's where you're wrong. In a previous statement, you said you had intercourse with Marilyn Boggs on the day of her murder. Are you standing by that statement?"

Barnet's tan lightened a few shades. "Well, I—I don't think so."

"Mr. Barnet, let me remind you that your previous statement is admissible in a court of law."

"I don't think we did."

"Are you lying now, or did you lie before? Which one is it, Mr. Barnet?"

"I'm not lying. It's hard to remember, that's all. It's been awhile."

Vargas said, "I'd remember the last time I had sexual relations with someone, especially if they ended up dead the same day."

It was well-put, but I didn't like hearing Mary Ann say it.

Barnet closed his eyes and stroked his Van Dyke before saying, "I think we did have, uh, sex that afternoon. Marilyn's death has been very tough on me. Maybe my brain is trying to blot things out."

"So, you did have intercourse with Marilyn Boggs the day she was found dead?"

"Yes."

"That's interesting, Mr. Barnet. You know why?"

A fly would shrug more noticeably than he did.

"Because the autopsy showed no evidence of intercourse."

"That's impossible."

"Nope, no semen, no abrasions, inflammation, nothing."

"I don't know how that can be."

I turned to Vargas. "What do you think? Maybe he's got a real tiny widgy."

Barnet shook his head.

Vargas said, "Is the reason you didn't have any relations that afternoon because you two were arguing?"

"Marilyn and I weren't arguing."

"We have a witness who gave a statement claiming you were."

"Witness? Gideon's no witness. He's the guy who did this, if you ask me."

"We're not asking you, Mr. Barnet."

"I'm just telling you what I think."

"You know what I think? I think you tried to hit up Mrs. Boggs for more money and an argument broke out. She was tired of giving you money."

"Giving me money?"

"Hold the baloney, Barnet. We know you hit her up for money before."

"And what makes you believe that?"

I stepped out onto a limb. "Marilyn confided in a friend. In fact, two of them."

"It was a loan, that's all. Nothing wrong with that."

"And nothing wrong when you overcharged her either?"

"I told you before, that was a mistake someone at the store made and it was paid back. As far as the loan is concerned, Marilyn was trying to help me through a rough patch."

"And when she refused to continue propping up your lifestyle and failing business, you threatened her, didn't you?"

Barnet's upper lip glistened. "That's not true."

"You filmed her in a sexually compromising way and threatened to embarrass her and the family, didn't you? You tried to blackmail her."

Fear flashed across Barnet's face. "I would never do something like that."

"You mean, you would never do something like that again?"

The slightest of pauses before he said, "Again?"

"Yes, again. We have two women willing to testify you did."

"It wasn't twi—"

Barnet stopped short, realizing he'd admitted to blackmailing at least once.

"You thought you could bully Marilyn into giving you money. You figured she had so much money she wouldn't risk the embarrassment of the film, illegally taken, that you took."

Barnet was silent.

Vargas said, "You were aware of the reputation clause in the trust, weren't you?"

"I have no idea what you're referring to."

I said, "When Marilyn Boggs resisted your blackmail attempt, you argued with her. When she wouldn't give in, you threatened her with a kitchen knife, didn't you?"

"No. I never did that."

"If you never did that, how do you explain the blood found on both the pants and the shirt you wore the day she died?"

"There wasn't any blood on my clothes."

"Not according to the forensics lab."

"Huh?"

"That's right, John. The lab identified the blood of Marilyn Boggs on your pants and shirt."

"But that's impossible."

I slid two photos marked up by the lab across the table. "They can pick up a microscopic spec of blood these days. It's really amazing."

Barnet's ears flattened and he shook the pictures.

"That brat came at me with a knife. I just reacted. I had no choice. I—I didn't mean to stab her; it was an accident." He tossed the photos back. "She should've just given me the money I needed. I couldn't lose the store. Marilyn knew that."

"Why don't you tell us what happened?"

Barnet drew a deep breath and exhaled. "I was in a hole this off-season. It was terrible. I needed money to keep things going, you know, buy some time until it turned around. But the spoiled brat wouldn't help me, even though it amounted to nothing to her."

"When she refused, you threatened her with the sex videos?"

Barnet shrugged. "I wasn't going to do nothing with them. It was just something to scare her with. But Marilyn just freaked out. Instead of just giving me the money I needed, she pulled a Wonder Woman thing and grabbed a knife off the counter." He shook his head. "You should've seen her standing there holding the knife. I laughed at her. Then she, she just snapped, started screaming and came at me like this." Barnet held his hand ear-height. "So, I grabbed her wrist, turning the knife away, but then she kneed me right in the balls."

"That's when you stabbed her?"

"It was self-defense. I'm telling you. In my wildest dreams I never thought she'd use it. I still can't believe it."

56

VARGAS LIVED IN A NICE COMMUNITY CALLED MARBELLA Lakes, off of Livingston. As I pulled into her driveway, the lightness in my belly intensified. The last time I felt like that was with Kayla at Baleens. That was a real date; this was just a celebratory dinner, wasn't it?

Mary Ann smiled as she got in the car. She had on those corduroy-type pants I liked. Did she know and wore them on purpose? Her perfume was some kind of floral one that made me think of nectar.

I said, "What time did you get off?"

"I left around four. The DA's office wanted me to run through the Sanchez file with ICE."

"They gonna deport him?"

"Yep. No sense spending the money and time prosecuting him, not to mention the cost to house in him prison for ten years."

"Maybe. I get it, but I don't totally buy into it. If you do the crime, you should do the time."

"It's an imperfect world, Frank."

"Tell me about it. How about Brighthouse? He plots to

kills his wife, and at the end of all this he gets twenty million."

Mary Ann said, "I still can't believe we almost pinned the murder on him. Without today's technology, we'd never have known the blood on his pants was two years old. Could you imagine putting him away for something he didn't do?"

I didn't need to imagine. The Barrow case had haunted me for almost ten years and flooded my head again.

"I'm sorry, Frank. I forgot about Barrow."

She could even read minds?

"It's okay. I don't think much about that case anymore. You helped me to see that I had to let it go."

"I'm glad you had the courage to move on."

Courage? Me?

"I don't know about courage, but let's change the subject, okay? Tonight, we celebrate! I still can't believe you've never been to Bleu Provence."

She smiled. "It's exciting to go to a new place. Thanks for putting it together."

"You're gonna love it."

"I'm sure I will."

"You know, Mary Ann, you look very nice tonight."

THE NEXT BOOK in this series is, Third Chances. Find it in eBook, Paperback, and Audio.

I hope you enjoyed reading this book as much as I enjoyed writing it. If you did, I'd appreciate if you would like a quick review on Amazon or your favorite book site. Reviews are an author's best friend and even a line or two is helpful. Thank you, Dan.

OTHER BOOKS BY DAN

Complicit Witness

Push Back

Ambition Cliff

You can keep abreast of my writing and have access to books that are free of discounting by joining my newsletter. It normally is out once a month and also contains notes on self- esteem, motivational pieces and wine articles.

It's free. See bottom of my website: www.danpetrosini.com

ABOUT THE AUTHOR

Dan is a USA Today and Amazon best-selling author who wrote his first story at the age of ten and enjoys telling a story or joke.

Dan gets his story ideas by exploring the question; What if?

In almost every situation he finds himself in, Dan explores what if this or that happened? What if this person died or did something unusual or illegal?

Dan's non-stop mind spin provides him with plenty of material to weave into interesting stories.

A fan of books and films that have twists and are difficult to predict, Dan crafts his stories to prevent readers from guessing correctly. He writes every day, forcing the words out when necessary and has written over twenty-five novels to date.

It's not a matter of wanting to write, Dan simply has to.

Dan passionately believes people can realize their dreams if they focus and act, and he encourages just that.

His favorite saying is – "The price of discipline is always less than the cost of regret"

Dan reminds people to get the negativity out of their lives. He believes it is contagious and advises people to steer clear of negative people. He knows having a true, positive mind set makes it feel like life is rigged in your favor. When he gets off base, he tells himself, 'You can't have a good day with a bad attitude.'

Married with two daughters and a needy Maltese, Dan lives in Southwest Florida. A New York native, Dan has taught at local colleges, writes novels, and plays tenor saxophone in several jazz bands. He also drinks way too much wine and never, ever takes himself too seriously.

He puts out a twice-a-month newsletter featuring articles, his writing and special deals and steals.

Sign up at www.danpetrosini.com

Made in United States
North Haven, CT
12 January 2024

47387810R00166